DEAD BY MIDNIGHT

An I-TEAM Christmas

by

Pamela Clare

DEAD BY MIDNIGHT

An I-Team Christmas

Published by Pamela Clare, 2015

Credits for cover images

Man with Pistol: Period Images

Background: Nattapong Sirilappanich/Depositphotos.com

Cover design by Carrie Divine/Seductive Designs

ISBN-10: 0990377148

ISBN-13: 978-0-9903771-4-6

DEDICATION

This book is dedicated to the victims of terrorism around the world and the courageous men and women who fight it.

ACKNOWLEDGEMENTS

Many thanks to Michelle White, Jackie Turner, Shell Ryan, Kim Eckenrode, and Pat Egan Fordyce for their typo wrangling and feedback as I worked on this novel.

A big hug and thanks to Andrea Ferrer for her help with Colombian Spanish.

Thanks to Christopher Wu for saying crazy shit that makes me laugh and for his feedback on certain law-enforcement elements of the story. Thanks to Benjamin Collins for his pilot's expertise. The two of you are like sons to me. Once, you were little kids. Now you help me with my books. How cool is that?

Special thanks to my dear son Benjamin Alexander for his unflagging support, firearms expertise, and his help getting this book out on time. What would I do without you?

I would also like to thank the wonderful and brilliant Kaylea Cross for allowing the hot alphas from her Hostage Rescue Team series to come play with my I-Team guys for a while. It was so much fun working with you.

Last but not least, thank you to the thousands of readers around the world who have made the I-Team series such a success over the past decade. Your love for these characters has inspired me, brought out the best in me as a writer, and made sharing their stories such an adventure. This book is for you.

CHAPTER ONE

Downtown Denver

December 19

14:10

Gabe Rossiter lay back on the gold damask coverlet and watched Kat unzip his fly, lifting his ass off the bed as she yanked down his trousers and boxer briefs, his cock already hard. "In a hurry?"

He sure as hell was.

"It's been *two weeks*." She pressed her hands to his chest for balance and straddled him, her party dress, hose, and panties tossed onto a nearby chair beside his prosthetic leg.

"Two weeks and two days." He'd been tempted to carve the days into their bathroom wall like a prisoner, a record of their involuntary celibacy as the parents of two—soon to be three—small children.

He had to hand it to himself. This had been a good idea. Drop the kids off with Kat's Uncle Allen and his wife. Surprise Kat with a room at the Palace Hotel. Get some nookie before the newspaper's annual bore-fest of a holiday party. Spend a night—an entire night—*alone* with his wife before the new baby came.

His fingers found the clasp of her bra, releasing the lacy fabric to expose her lush breasts, their nipples dark from pregnancy. He took their weight in his hands, teased their velvety tips with his thumbs, gratified by the tremor that ran through her.

She pressed her breasts deeper into his hands, closed her eyes, her nipples drawing tight. He let himself play, enjoying it every bit as much as she did. Her breathing turned to whimpers, then to soft moans, making him harder.

He reached down with one hand to tease her clit.

"*Yes.*" Her head fell back, her long, dark hair tickling his thighs, the curve of her rounded belly adding to her femininity, making her even sexier in his eyes.

"You are so beautiful."

But she was too lost in sensation to hear him.

Good.

Her hips began to move, little involuntary jerks that told him she was fast moving toward orgasm, her breath unraveling in sweet little moans. Then her head came up, and she looked down at him through dilated pupils. "I want you inside me. *Now.*"

Yes, this had been a *very* good idea.

Gabe grasped his cock and held it as she raised herself up and then lowered herself onto him, taking all of him into her tight, wet heat.

Oh, yeah.

Pleasure jolted through him, and his eyes drifted shut.

He jerked them open again, not wanting to miss a moment of this.

"*Gabe.*" She whispered his name, her eyes closing as she began to move, her hips rocking against him.

He fought the urge to thrust, willed himself to hold still, letting her take what she needed from him.

God, he loved her—loved her, cherished her, needed her. He wasn't sure how it was possible, but he loved her more than he had when he'd married her almost four years ago. She'd saved him from himself, forgiven him when he hadn't deserved it. She'd given him children. She'd brought joy back into his life.

She *was* life.

Her breath came in pants now as she ground herself against him, her eyes squeezed shut, her nails digging into his chest, her thighs drawing tight against his hips. She came with a cry, her back arching, her inner muscles clenching around him. He found himself moaning, too, so aroused he thought his balls might burst.

He stayed with her, giving her time to savor the pleasure, the spasms inside her slowly subsiding, her breathing gradually returning to normal. He watched her as the tension drained from her body, leaving her almost limp.

She opened her eyes and gave him a smile that made his pulse skip.

"Welcome back, beautiful." He reached up, brushed the hair from her cheek.

She laughed, slid her palms over his chest. "I needed that."

He grinned, gave a little thrust with his hips, his cock aching and still buried inside her. "There's more where that came from."

"Mmm. I hope so." She raised herself off him, his cock falling free, its length glistening with her wetness.

Gabe watched as she turned and got onto her hands and knees, giving him a rear view that sent lust shearing through his belly. He rose onto his knees, moved up behind her, stroked her. And then he just had to taste.

KAT GASPED, SHOCKED BY the hot swipe of Gabe's tongue. Oh, but he knew *just* how to love her. He teased her with flicks of his tongue, caught her inner lips with his mouth, sucked on her clitoris, one sweet sensation colliding with the next. "*Oh, yes.*"

He moaned, the sound vibrating through her. "You taste so good."

He kept up his assault until she was fully aroused and aching, erotic pleasure shivering through her. Then he shifted into position behind her, and she spread her legs wider, eager to feel him inside her again.

He entered her with a single, smooth thrust, groaning her name. "*Kat.*"

They fit together so perfectly, two halves that made a perfect whole. His cock filled her, stretched her, stroked every inch of her all the way to the mouth of her womb, his hands caressing the skin of her back, her buttocks, her hips. He bent over her, reached between her legs to tease her clit, his lips pressing hot kisses to her shoulders, his hips thrusting faster as the urgency between them began to build.

She gave herself over to his loving, nothing in her world but him, his body conjuring magic from hers, bliss already building toward another orgasm, leaving her mindless. It felt so good ... *so* good ... stroke after slick stroke ... stretching her, filling her ... feeding that sweet ache.

And then she was there, suspended somewhere between heaven and earth, hovering on the radiant edge of another climax. Her breath caught ... and she came again in a wave of perfect bliss, the pleasure blinding.

She cried out, an almost incoherent rush of words in her native Navajo welling up from inside her, ending with the most important words of all. "*Ayor anosh'ni!*"

I love you.

Yes, she loved him—this man, her lover, her half-side. She might have loved him since before she'd been born, the two of them made for each other.

"*Kat.*" He whispered her name, keeping his rhythm steady, making her pleasure last, his lips leaving a trail of hot kisses on her back.

He always put her pleasure first, but now it was time for him to claim his own. His hands moved to grasp her hips, and he let himself go, his thrusts coming faster and harder until he was driving into her. His fingers dug into her hips, his breathing ragged, his restraint shattered.

He came with a groan, finishing with a few powerful strokes, spilling himself inside her. For a moment, they stayed like that, bodies still joined, hearts still pounding, the mingled scents of salt and musk filling her head.

Then Gabe drew her back with him, spooning her in his arms, their heads resting on thick pillows. He felt so solid behind her, his body firm and strong. And for a time they lay together in the stillness, savoring the moment, his fingertips tracing lines over her skin, their heartbeats slowing.

"What time does that damned party start?" His voice was deep, husky.

She glanced at the clock on the nightstand, saw that it was almost five. "Seven."

"What if we make a fashionably late entrance?"

She turned in his arms to face him, tucking one of her legs between his thighs. "We can't be late. Matt is bringing Holly as his plus-one."

"Seriously?"

"Yes." She couldn't help but smile.

Gabe chuckled. "I can see why you wouldn't want to miss that."

"That still gives us almost two hours."

"Two hours." He brushed his lips over hers, smiled. "I bet we can find some way to keep busy till then."

18:30

MARC HUNTER PICKED A black tie out of the closet then turned to face Sophie. He wished they were going on a date instead of heading to this stupid holiday party, because—*damn*—she looked good enough to eat. A cocktail gown of black beaded silk clung to her curves, her strawberry blond hair done up in a twist. But, no, they were going to waste the entire evening—and all that sexy—on the newspaper.

"Every year I swear we won't go to this damned party again next year, but every year we go. We don't need the money."

The newspaper's publisher traditionally passed out holiday bonuses at the party—the paper's way of blackmailing staff into attending. Anyone who didn't show up at the party had to wait until their first paycheck in January to get their bonus. Most people depended on that check to buy Christmas gifts for their loved ones. But Marc earned a decent salary as captain of the Denver Police Department's SWAT team. They weren't living from paycheck to paycheck.

Sophie smiled up at him, took the tie from his hands, went to work with it. "Matt is bringing Holly as his guest, and I can't wait to see Tom's face."

Marc must not have heard right. "Matt is bringing *Holly*?"

Sophie nodded.

"Does Nick know?"

Nick Andris was Holly's husband of almost a year. A former CIA paramilitary officer, he'd take poor Matt Harker apart if he thought the man was hot on his wife.

Sophie rolled her eyes. "Of course he knows. He's busy tonight—some important meeting. He thought the idea of Holly crashing the party was funny."

"What's to stop Tom from throwing her out?"

"It's the holiday party. You know—peace on Earth, good will to people, God bless us every one." She adjusted the knot she'd made, drew it tight. "Besides, he wouldn't want to cause a scene and embarrass the new publisher."

Marc wasn't convinced. "Since when does Tom care about making a scene?"

"Ever since the publisher told him the I-Team was too expensive and might get cut from the budget."

Marc caught his wife's hands. "What? When did this happen?"

The I-Team—or Investigative Team—was made up of the best reporters on the paper's staff. They did the sort of old-fashioned digging that turned up the big stories, the kind that brought down the assholes and changed state laws. It was Sophie's work as an I-Team reporter that had freed Marc from spending the rest of his life in a prison cell.

She ran her hand down his tie, smoothed it into place. "Tom told us about it in Monday's I-Team meeting."

Marc slid his fingers through hers. "Why didn't you say anything?"

"It's almost Christmas. I didn't want to worry you. Besides, it doesn't make sense to get upset about something that might not happen."

He drew her into his arms. "Hey, I'm your husband, remember? Don't keep things like that from me. It's my job to carry half the burden."

He knew it wasn't the loss of income that worried her, but the prospect of losing a job she loved. God knew she had to love the work to put up with her dick of a boss.

Marc had never cared for the way Tom Trent treated his staff.

Sophie kissed his cheek. "I don't want to think about it. Let's just enjoy tonight."

Marc grabbed his loaded SIG P239 and slipped it into its custom leather pocket holster, then shoved both into his trouser pocket with his badge. "Is Rossiter coming?"

Sophie crossed the room, picked up the sparkly black handbag she'd bought to go with her gown. "Yes, of course."

Well, that was something. He and Rossiter, who'd once worked in law enforcement as a park ranger, could shoot the shit, catch up on the latest, and commiserate. There was safety in numbers.

"And, Marc, guess what else will be coming to the party."

Marc looked up in time to see Sophie lift her gown. Beneath the silk and glitter, she was wearing black stockings, black lace garters—and nothing else. Her delicious ass was bare, along with all those sweet little female bits between her thighs.

Holy hell.

Marc's pulse skipped, blood surging to his groin.

She settled the black lace of her gown into place, her lips curving in a sexy smile. "Are you coming?"

Oh, he wouldn't miss this for the world.

18:55

REECE SHERIDAN TURNED THE corner into the Palace Hotel's massive parking garage and drew their Lexus RX to a stop, leaving the keys in the ignition for the valet. He walked around to the passenger side and opened the door for his wife, the cold biting through his tux.

Kara stepped out, looking gorgeous in a long gown of midnight blue velvet, a matching velvet wrap around her shoulders, her dark hair pulled back to hang down her back. "Are you sure I'm dressed up enough?"

"You look perfect." He kissed her cheek.

She wasn't comfortable with this kind of black-tie affair. Then again, neither was he. It certainly wasn't why he'd run for office. But Governor Thyfault's wife was in the hospital recovering from an appendectomy, so it was Reece's job as lieutenant governor to attend the annual British Consulate General's Christmas party.

A young man in a hotel uniform approached, handed Reece a ticket.

Reece tipped him with a ten. "Happy holidays."

"Thanks." The kid smiled, then slipped into the car and drove away.

Reece tucked his arm through Kara's and hurried with her toward the front entrance, its brass-trimmed doors flanked by uniformed doormen.

"When you introduce me to him, I call him 'Your Excellency,' but after that I can just say 'Sir' or 'Mr. Ambassador'?"

"You can use either interchangeably. You also call him Ambassador DeLacy."

"What about the Secretary of State?"

"Madam Secretary will do—or Secretary Holmes." He gave her arm a little tug. "Would you relax? You'll probably spend most of the evening bored to tears."

"I don't want to embarrass you."

"Hey, don't worry about that. You could never let me down."

He hated to think she was nervous. His career demanded much more sacrifice from her than hers required of him. She'd attended endless parties, helped him write speeches, stood by him during election campaigns. She'd spent too many nights putting the kids to bed by herself because he was working late. She'd endured the risks associated with having a husband in public office. Through it all, she had never once complained.

Reece was a lucky bastard, and he knew it.

One of the doormen opened the door, choir music drifting on a rush of warm air. "Welcome to the Palace Hotel."

"Thank you." Reece handed each of them a ten. "Happy holidays."

The doorman grinned. "Thank you, sir. Happy holidays to you, too."

They stepped inside, and Kara gave a little cry, gazing around them with wide eyes. "Isn't it beautiful?"

The Palace Hotel was famous for its historic décor, which it brought to life every holiday season with the most spectacular Christmas decorations in the city. The hotel's eight-story-high atrium glittered from the floor to the very top with white lights, the arches of the mezzanine level and the massive chandelier decorated with light strands, pine boughs, and red ribbon. In the center of the atrium stood a tall Christmas tree, its top rising to the mezzanine level, its branches decorated with white lights and hundreds of delicate blown glass ornaments that were probably antique. A children's choir stood in white robes and red sashes off to one side of the lobby, singing "Silent Night," a fire burning in the big fireplace nearby.

Kara stopped to take it all in. "It's like something from a postcard."

"Yes, it is." Reece leaned down, spoke for her ears alone. "I'd hate to pay their December electricity bill."

She laughed. "Don't be such a Grinch."

Reece was familiar with the hotel and guided Kara to a bank of elevators that led to the mezzanine and the Grand Ballroom. He withdrew the formal printed invitation from his pocket, knowing security would stop them outside the ballroom.

A voice came from behind them. "I guess they let anyone in this place."

They both turned and saw Joaquin Ramirez, the *Denver Independent*'s Pulitzer Prize-winning photographer, walking up behind them. He was dressed in a sharp black tux, black bowtie at his throat, heavy camera bag slung over his shoulder.

Kara and Ramirez were old friends. They had worked together at the paper until she'd married Reece. Now she worked as a freelance journalist, writing articles for big papers and magazines, while Ramirez still worked for the paper.

"Hey, good to see you." Reece reached out, shook Ramirez's hand.

Kara kissed his cheek. "I didn't know you were coming."

Ramirez looked confused. "I always come to the holiday party."

"Oh!" Kara laughed. "The Indie is having its holiday party here tonight?"

Ramirez nodded. "Isn't that why you're here?"

"We're going to the British Consulate General's Christmas party."

"Fancy." Ramirez grinned. "Baird, the new publisher, wants me to take photos. Harker is bringing Holly. I want to get a shot of Tom's face when he sees her."

"Seriously?" Kara laughed. "That's the best thing I've heard all day. I wish I could see that."

She looked hopefully over at Reece. "Maybe we can pop in and say hello to everyone."

Reece shrugged. "I don't see why not."

He had to fight back a grin at the relief on her face.

19:00

JOSÉ "PEPE" ROJAS MORENO parked the Lexus, got out, and lit up a cigarette, the bastard's ten-dollar bill still in his hand. The stupid *hijueputa* thought he was so generous, so powerful. He would never understand real money or true power.

Pepe had recognized him immediately as Reece Sheridan, the state's lieutenant governor, one of the top names on the list. The bastard would find out soon enough that he had power over nothing, not even his life.

Pepe made his way back down toward the entrance, not giving a damn if his boss caught him smoking and fired him. This job had only ever been the means to an end, a way of getting to know his way around Denver and the hotel. After tonight, he would no longer need it. Either he'd had leave this freezing cold city and head back to the warmth of Colombia—or he'd be dead.

Ahead of him, well-dressed couples made their way toward the hotel's front entrance. Slowly, two by two, the rats were walking into the trap. He felt nothing but contempt for them.

Hijueputas. Comemierdas. Malparidos.

Sons of whores. Shit-eaters. Bastards.

Some were laughing and smiling, oblivious to what awaited them. Others seemed to be angry or worried. But the fears that oppressed them at this moment were petty compared to what lay ahead of them.

He had planned this for more than a year, moving men into position, getting the arms, ammo, and explosives he'd need. He was the nephew of La Culebra, and he wouldn't let his uncle or his cousin down, even if he had to kill every man, woman, and child here. Even if he had to die.

He glanced down at his watch.

The fun was about to begin.

CHAPTER TWO

19:00

"What's wrong?"

"Nothing's wrong," Holly Andris lied.

She usually had no trouble hiding her feelings from people, but tonight she was failing miserably.

Matt Harker turned the car into the hotel's parking garage. "I might not be a super-spy like you are, but I can tell you're feeling down."

"I'm not a spy. I was never a spy. I'm an intelligence expert." She hoped Matt would drop it.

He didn't. "Yeah, whatever. Something has you upset."

Journalists could be *such* a pain in the butt.

"Nick and I got into a fight."

"Don't the two of you bicker a lot?"

"Yes, but not like this." The whole thing had left her feeling sick, their last words to each other running through her mind on a loop.

"You're thirty-five, Holly. I'm almost forty. If we're going to have kids, we need to start soon."

"That's easy for you to say. You're not the one who has to go through it. All you have to do is come."

Well, it was true, wasn't it? The male contribution to reproduction was unimpressive compared to that of females—unless you were a seahorse.

"I can't change human biology, but if you think I'd leave you to face it by yourself, you're wrong. I'm not that kind of man."

"Lots of women have babies in their forties."

"How many of them do it without medical intervention? How many face complications as a result of their age?"

"I'm not ready."

"Okay. When will you be ready?"

"I don't know."

"Yeah? Well, maybe you need to rethink your priorities."

He'd seemed so angry. She hadn't been able to tell him that she was afraid.

What if something went wrong? What if she turned out to be like her mother? Or, worse yet, her father?

No kid deserved that.

Besides, having something the size of a baby come out of her vagina seemed like a very bad idea. She hated pain.

Matt stopped his car, put it into park. "Whatever it was, I'm sure you'll move beyond it. Nick is crazy about you."

"I hope you're right." She and Nick hadn't had time to resolve the argument before he'd had to leave for his conference call with Javier and the Pentagon, and she'd left home bleeding inside. The last thing she wanted to do was disappoint Nick or make him worry that he'd married the wrong woman. She knew how ugly divorce could be. Her parents had spent more time cheating on one another and fighting in court than they'd spent married. She couldn't let her marriage turn out like theirs.

Matt looked over at Holly, his hand on the door handle. "Are you ready?"

Holly took in a breath, released it, doing her best to set her emotions aside. She smiled. "I've waited a long time for this."

Holly had worked for the *Denver Independent* as an entertainment writer until two summers ago when a corrupt CIA officer had tried to have her killed, his actions exposing her role as a non-cover officer for the Agency. Tom Trent, the paper's editor, had been furious to discover that an operative had been working in his newsroom and had fired her, even though her work as a reporter had been outstanding and her job for the government had never entailed spying on the paper.

At first, she'd been crushed, but life after journalism had turned out much better than she could have imagined. She and Nick had both gone to work for Cobra International Solutions, a black-ops firm owned by Javier Corbray and Derek Tower. She often worked side by side with Nick, traveling the world with him on what felt like a grand adventure.

There was no revenge sweeter than success, and she was here to show Tom that her life was good without his newspaper—better, even.

She stepped out of the warm car into the freezing cold and hurried over to Matt, hugging her cropped coat of faux white mink tightly around herself. "Let me fix that tie."

He glanced down. "It's fine."

Holly shook her head. "What would you know?"

For the decade she'd known him, Matt had looked like he dressed out of his laundry basket, his shirts and slacks wrinkled, his one-and-only tie crumpled. As it turned out, he *did* dress out of his laundry basket. Holly had taken it upon herself to rent his tux, wanting to make sure he looked his best.

He was her "date" for the night, after all.

"Are you ready?" Shivering, she stepped back, looked him up and down, and was pleased with what she saw.

Clean-shaven, his hair combed, and wearing Armani, Matt was a surprisingly handsome man.

"Are you kidding? I can't wait to see Tom's face." Matt slipped his arm around her shoulders. "Let's get you inside before you freeze to death."

"Good idea."

At their approach, both doormen jumped forward, opening the doors.

"Good evening, miss," said one.

Holly flashed them both a smile. "Thank you."

Matt tipped them, then took Holly's arm, a grin on his face. "They couldn't take their eyes off you."

But Holly barely heard him, her gaze fixed on the beautiful Christmas decorations, the scene like something from an age gone by. Some of her sadness slipped away, warmth chasing away the chill.

Matt leaned down, spoke for her ears alone. "Men are staring at you."

"What? Oh." She'd put some effort into her appearance tonight, choosing a short illusion slip dress of champagne-colored silk with strategically placed black and gold beading by Basix Black Label and paired it with strappy Manolo Blahnik heels in gold.

Matt chuckled. "You might be used to that, but it's a new experience for me."

She smiled up at him. "We need to find someone for you."

"With *you* on my arm?" He laughed again. "Not gonna happen."

Matt's wife had divorced him the same crazy summer that Holly had met Nick, and he hadn't yet gotten back into dating. She knew it was probably hard for a man who was almost fifty to put himself out there, but she was determined to help him do just that. If tonight helped bolster his confidence, so much the better.

They headed up the wide staircase—Holly thought it allowed for a better entrance than a crowded elevator—then checked their jackets with the cloakroom, and made their way along the wide mezzanine balcony toward the Onyx Room.

Matt glanced through the door of the Grand Ballroom. "I wonder what's happening in there? Check it out. They've got a chamber orchestra, decorations up the wazoo, armed security."

Holly glanced over, saw Ambassador DeLacy, who looked distinguished as always, and Secretary Holmes, who'd ditched the ubiquitous beige pantsuit for a long gown of black velvet. "It's the British Consulate's annual Christmas party. Oh, hey, Kara and Reece are here."

She would have to stop in later to say hello.

For now, she needed to focus on her mission.

They stopped at the table outside the Onyx Room, where a woman with a list of staff was checking off names.

Matt held out his employee ID. "Matt Harker, plus one."

Holly smiled at the woman, gave Matt's arm a squeeze, grateful that he was giving her this chance.

"Here goes," he said.

He stepped back, motioned her toward the door. She lifted her chin, smiled, and walked into the Onyx Room as if she owned the place.

The onyx pillars for which the room had been named had been decorated with pine garlands and white lights, elaborate ceiling moldings framing a domed painting of naked cherubs, who seemed to stare down on them with delight.

Holly spotted her I-Team friends seated at a table to the right of the bar—Sophie and Marc, Kat and Gabe, Joaquin, and Alex Carmichael. Joaquin got to his feet when he saw her, camera in hand, a conspiratorial grin on his face.

Tom stood not far from them, scotch in hand, talking with a balding man Holly assumed was the new publisher. He had the look of a man who considered it his birthright to tell other people what to do.

She waved to her friends and made her way toward the bar. She knew the moment Tom spotted her. His head came around, and his face turned red. She smiled as she passed him, tickling his jaw with her manicured fingertips, her gaze meeting his.

She let her voice go husky. "Hi, Tom. Nice party."

From nearby came muffled laughter and the whir of Joaquin's camera.

19:15

MARC LEFT ROSSITER AT the buffet and walked up behind Sophie where she stood talking with Holly. He touched his hand to her waist and whispered in her ear. "Let's get the hell out of here."

Ever since he'd gotten a glimpse of what she was and wasn't wearing beneath that little black dress, all he'd been able to think about was getting his hands on her.

She shook her head. "We can't leave yet. Baird hasn't passed out bonus checks. If we leave before he does, he won't remember I was here."

Shit.

"I've got some important business to attend to." He dropped his voice to a whisper again, nuzzled her ear. *"Between your legs."*

Her cheeks flushed pink. "Now?"

"Come on." Not bothering to wait for her to finish her conversation, he took her hand and led her out of the door and along the balcony.

"Where are we going?"

"To find someplace private."

"What?" She stopped in her tracks.

He turned, bent down, and kissed her. "Right now, all I can think about is how very much I want to fuck you, so either we find someplace nice and private, or this will be remembered as the most awkward holiday party ever."

"You're out of your mind." She laughed, shook her head. But her pupils had dilated, and the smile wouldn't leave her face.

She wanted him, too.

He set off again, the thought of burying himself inside her making it hard to think of anything else. But that's how it was. Once a person had sex on the brain, the only way to find relief was to fuck. "There has to be an empty conference room or linen closet or powder room around here."

"I don't want to end up in tomorrow's arrest reports."

"Neither do I." It wouldn't look good for a high-ranking city cop to be caught having public sex, even with his wife. Chief Irving would have his ass.

They came to a door labeled Marble Room but found it locked. A little further down, they discovered a janitor's closet. Though it was unlocked, the door was slatted and would give anyone who passed a clear view. They'd be arrested for sure.

"Maybe we should see if they have any vacant rooms," Sophie said.

"I don't think this is a pay-by-the-hour kind of place."

They went around the corner and found themselves in a service hallway behind the Grand Ballroom, the narrow space crowded with busy hotel staff and security. Marc was about to suggest they go out to the car when Sophie tugged on his hand.

"Over there." She pointed to a family restroom.

They found the door unlocked.

Marc drew Sophie inside with him, locked the door behind them.

Automatic lights flickered on, revealing a small anteroom with an antique leather wingback chair and a coffee table that held a vase of roses. Beyond stood a restroom with a white marble basin and floor, a brass changing table, and a single restroom stall.

"I bet this is for nursing moms."

"I don't care if it's for masturbating extraterrestrials." He turned Sophie toward the chair, desire for her thrumming in his veins. "Bend over."

She did as he asked, grasping the chair's arms, wiggling her ass, looking over her shoulder at him. "*Hurry.*"

He rucked up her cocktail dress, the breath rushing from his lungs as he took in the sight of her—dark garters against her creamy, pale skin, her rounded ass, the rosy slash of her exposed pussy. "You are so fucking *hot.*"

He reached down, explored that tender flesh. She was already wet, the scent of her making his pulse pound. He teased her clit, slid a finger inside her, stroking her. He wanted this to be as good for her as it would be for him.

His Sophie. His sprite. His wife.

Where would he be without her?

He loved her, would never stop loving her. She was his beginning and his end. She'd believed in him when the world had turned against him and he'd no longer believed in himself. She'd risked her career and her life for him. Though he could never be the man he'd set out to become, he tried every day to be the man she deserved—both in and out of bed. He'd made it his business to know how to please her, how to make her scream, how to satisfy her completely.

Already, her breath was coming faster, her wetness drenching his fingers.

She moaned. "I want you inside me."

He forced her feet apart with his. "Spread your legs wider."

He grasped a rounded hip with one hand and his cock with the other, then teased her with the engorged head, rubbing it against her cleft, nudging the tip inside her, then withdrawing again.

She whimpered. "Stop teasing me."

It was torture for him, too. His cock ached to go deep, his blood humming with lust, his mind focused on one thing.

Sophie.

He bent over her, kissed her neck, nipped the sensitive skin of her nape. "You're going to spend the rest of the night with me dripping out of you."

And he would spend the rest of the night with her scent all over him.

Perfect.

She whimpered in frustration, arching her lower back. "*Please.*"

He entered her with a single, slow thrust that made them both moan, then held himself still inside her, giving himself time to harness his self-control. He wanted to take this slowly, wanted to make it last.

A quick fuck didn't have to be a *fast* fuck, after all.

He willed himself to relax, then began to move, savoring the feel of her, her sweet pussy gripping him like a fist.

Oh, God, yes.

Now *this* was a party.

19:22

CHARLES BAIRD, THE NEW publisher, was every bit as self-centered and arrogant as Holly had believed he would be. He also loved to hear himself talk. She'd met so many men like him over the years.

"Profitability is key to my—"

"I completely agree." Holly interrupted him, afraid she'd drift into a coma if she didn't shut him up. "Newspapers are businesses first and foremost. The paper has to remain profitable to survive, and that means someone has to make tough decisions."

"*I* am that someone, as I'm sure you know." He seemed gratified by her response, his gaze dropping to her breasts once again. "Take the I-Team, for example. We are now the only paper in Colorado to have a team of reporters dedicated to old-school investigative reporting. It's expensive and inefficient—"

"And such a smart investment on your part." She willed herself to look deeply into his flat brown eyes. "It takes genius to see the deeper value of something."

Charles was not a genius, but he certainly liked to think he was.

Before he could respond, she went on.

"The other papers have given up investigative journalism because it's expensive. They've made the short-sighted mistake of turning to wire copy, and now they all carry the same stories. They've sacrificed what made them a unique product to save money. It has cost them their edge and lost them readership." She plucked an imaginary piece of lint off his lapel, smiled up at him. "People pick up *your* paper because they know they'll read something they can't find anywhere else. It must have been a hard decision, but I think you did the right thing—purely from a business perspective, of course."

He looked confused for a moment, then nodded, his gaze dropping to her breasts again. "You've got a good head for business, Ms. Andris."

"Thank you, Charles." Holly's work here was done. *Too easy.* "If you'll excuse me for just a moment, I need to visit the powder room."

He smiled. "When you get back, I'll buy you a drink, and we can talk more about my vision for the paper."

What a narcissist!

She didn't plan to spend another moment in his company, but she didn't say this, of course. She smiled, touched a hand to his arm. "I can't wait."

Relieved to be free of him, she turned and walked out of the room, hoping Kara and Reece were still at the British Consulate's party. She decided against trying to enter through the main doors, instead taking the service hallway. She'd have a better chance of sneaking into the party through the Grand Ballroom's back entrance.

She passed a family restroom, heard moaning. Was someone in trouble?

She slowed down, listened.

The rhythmic *bonk* of something hitting the wall again and again. Muffled moans. And then a woman crying out.

"Oh, God, Marc!"

Sophie?

There was a time and a place for sex, and it sounded to Holly like Sophie and her hunk of a husband had found both the time and the place.

Fighting not to laugh, Holly glanced over her shoulder—and collided with a server pushing a draped cart.

"Excuse me!" she said. "I guess I should watch where I'm going."

The server glared at her, his hand jerking on the drapery, but not before she saw what he was trying to hide.

Jutting from beneath a white cloth was the wooden stock of an AK.

Her adrenaline spiked—and then her training kicked in.

Freaking perfect.

She buried her shock, smiled. "I think I've had a bit too much to drink. Is this the Onyx Room?"

She could smell his fear, knew he was hovering between the hope that she hadn't seen and the impulse to strike out at her.

Questions raced through her mind. Who was his intended target? What else did he have hidden on that cart? Would he open fire here and now? Was he here by himself, or had he arrived with friends?

Sweat beaded on his forehead, but he answered her question. "No, the room you want is that way."

His accent was Spanish.

She gave him a bright smile. "Thanks! I got all turned around."

She turned and walked with a slight wobble back the way she'd come, certain he was watching her. She needed to warn security, warn her friends.

She turned toward the Onyx Room, glancing back to see whether he'd followed her. The moment she was certain she was out of sight, she ran up to the security guards that flanked the entrance to the ballroom.

She kept her voice calm. "Get Ambassador DeLacy, Secretary Holmes, and the Lt. Governor out of here *now*. Clear the room. There's a man dressed as a server with an AK. He's in the service hallway, and the weapon is hidden on a service cart."

The guards looked at each other, then back at Holly.

"Who are you? Who do you work for?"

"We don't have time for this!" Holly typed a group text to Sophie, Kat, and Kara.

Get out now! Danger. There's a man dressed as a server with an AK and—

"What are you doing?"

Before she could finish the message, one of the guards took her cell phone. She fought to hold onto it, just managing to hit "Send" before he tore it from her hands.

"You won't listen to me, but they will." She spoke while he read what she'd typed. "I'm Holly Andris. I'm an operative with Cobra International Solutions, a private security firm. Give me back my phone."

The security guard handed it back, then spoke into his mic. "We've got a woman here who says she saw a man with an assault rifle in the service hallway. She says he was dressed as a waiter. She claims to work for a security firm called Cobra."

While he wasted precious minutes, Holly called 911. "There's a man with an assault rifle outside the Grand Ballroom at the Palace Hotel."

"What is your name, ma'am?"

"Sorry, but I don't have time to chat." She called Nick, which is what she ought to have done in the first place. He could pull strings higher up the flagpole than the 911 dispatcher and make things happen more quickly.

He answered on the third ring. "What is it? I can't talk right—"

He was still angry, but that didn't matter.

"Call the police. Tell them to mobilize SWAT. I just ran into a man pretending to be a server who has smuggled an AK into the hotel. He had it hidden beneath a drape on a service cart."

"Get out. Now."

"The British Consulate General is hosting its annual Christmas party, and the Secretary of State is here. We need SWAT right away. I warned security, but I don't think they believe me."

"Get the hell out of there *now*, before—"

Holly saw *him*. "Oh, my God."

The assailant was standing not twenty feet away from her, watching her, panic on his face, an AKM with a thirty-round magazine in his hands.

He raised the weapon.

"Everyone get down!" The guard drew his sidearm. "Drop your weapon!"

The AK opened up.

Rat-at-at-at! Rat-at-at-at! Rat-at-at-at!

Screams. Shouts. The answering blast of the guard's firearm.

Bam! Bam! Bam!

Holly's instinct was to hit the floor, but she couldn't take cover, not yet, not with so many lives at stake. On a burst of adrenaline, she dashed across the hallway, her cell phone falling from her hands, bullets sending up a spray of plaster from the walls around her, people lying on the floor, terror on their faces.

Shit!

Heart thrumming, she reached out—and pulled the fire alarm.

Blinding pain exploded against her skull.

And then ... nothing.

CHAPTER THREE

19:28

"Holly?" Nick Andris heard the rattle of the AK, found himself on his feet, shouting into his cell phone. "Holly!"

"What is it, man?" Javier Corbray, his boss, looked down at him from the viewscreen on the wall.

Nick's heart hammered, adrenaline scattering his thoughts. "There's an active shooter at the Palace Hotel. Holly said she'd seen a man with an AK. He was pretending to be a server. Then she said, 'Oh, my God,' and the shooter opened fire."

"What the …?"

Nick's mind raced. Had she been shot? What had her last words meant? Had the shooter aimed his weapon at her?

The thought sickened him. He'd almost lost her once already.

If she'd been shot…

No.

He fought to control his emotions. He didn't have time for fear. Holly—and everyone else at the hotel—needed him to take action. "She said the British Consulate General is hosting a party, and the Secretary of State is there. I'm calling police dispatch."

"I'll call the White House."

Nick made the call, identified himself, reported what he'd been told. From the viewscreen speakers, he could hear Corbray sharing the basics with the president's chief of staff, who would probably turn it all over to the FBI.

"Are you at the scene?" dispatch asked.

"No. My wife is there. She called me. I heard gunshots over the phone." It took all his self-control not to shout.

"We're getting other calls coming in. I've taken down your information, sir, but because you're not at the scene, I'm letting you go."

"Thanks." Nick ended the call, reached for the remote, looked up at the camera. "I'm going to the Palace Hotel to get Holly."

"Wait, bro, you can't just go charging in—"

Nick ended the video conference, cutting Corbray off mid-sentence. He left the conference room and ran to his weapons locker, Holly's last words to him echoing in his mind, panic coiling with dread and a sense of helplessness in his gut.

He'd been short with her today, saying things he regretted, and now...

Now he might never get the chance to apologize.

Fuck that.

She would be okay. She had to be okay.

He entered the combination to his locker and jerked it open, trading his suit and tie for night BDUs, weapons, and a bag of tactical gear. He skipped the elevator and took the stairs two at a time down to the parking garage.

He heard squealing tires and saw Derek Tower, his other boss and co-owner of Cobra, speeding toward him in one of the company's bullet-proof

SUVs. Tower drew to a stop in front of him, threw open the passenger side door. "Corbray called. Let's go."

19:28

PEPE HEARD THE GUNFIRE, the screams, the wail of the fire alarm.

¡Coño!

Not yet! It wasn't time!

Something had gone wrong. No one was supposed to move until 19:30. The plan was to close in on the hotel all at once from all directions, blocking the exits to make certain no one got out.

Now, people flooded out the hotel's front doors, men, women, and children, some screaming, some crying, their faces pinched by fear.

"Man, someone's firing a gun," one of the other valets said. "I'm getting the fuck out of here."

Then security guards in black suits pushed their way through the throng, guiding the British ambassador out to the limo that pulled up to the curb.

And like that, one of their three prime hostages was gone.

In the distance, he heard sirens.

Either they acted now, or this past year would be a waste, and his uncle...

¡Madre de Dios!

His uncle would cut him to pieces—or worse, throw him to the snakes.

Pepe swore, grabbed his cell phone, and typed in a text message, sent a group SMS to his men.

Vamos a rumbear.

Let's party.

19:28

MARC COVERED SOPHIE'S BODY with his own, his pants still down around his knees, his nervous system caught between sexual climax and an adrenaline rush. Gunshots pierced the unholy din of the fire alarm. There were two shooters—one with what sounded like an AK-47 and the other with some kind of high-caliber semi-auto. The second was almost certainly one of the security guards.

Whoever had tripped the alarm deserved a medal. It would bring the fire department and ambulances to treat the wounded, and it would also bring the DPD. But what they really needed was Marc's team. They needed SWAT.

He thrust his hand in his pocket, drew out his cell, dialed Chief Irving. "It's Hunter. We've got an active shooter at the Palace Hotel. I say again, an active shooter at the Palace Hotel. Mobilize my team."

"I copy Hunter. Are you armed?"

"Yes, but I'm not in the same room as the shooter." He filled Irving in, telling him everything he knew.

"Stay on the line while I call dispatch."

"Copy that." Marc waited.

Irving was back in a blink. "Dispatch says they've already received several calls. I've mobilized SWAT. I'll let the Denver office of the FBI know, too, in case we're looking at a hostage grab. The troops are on their way."

Then, as abruptly as it had started, the shooting stopped.

"It stopped."

"See what you can find out. And Hunter?"

"Yeah?"

"I'm officially placing you on duty. You'll be our eyes and ears."

"Do I get paid OT for this?"

"Smartass."

"Copy that. I'll get back to you."

Not certain whether the shooting was truly over, Marc got to his feet, helped Sophie to stand, then yanked up his pants and zipped his fly. "Lock the door behind me, then go into the bathroom stall, shut the door, and crouch down in the back corner. Make yourself into as small a target as possible. Don't come out until I call for you."

She looked up at him through terrified blue eyes, her face pale. "Wh-what are you going to do?"

He hated the son of a bitch who'd put fear in her heart.

"I'm going to find out what's going on." He slipped out of his dinner jacket and cummerbund and handed both to her. "Get in there, and stay put. Got it?"

"Yes. But Hunt?"

"Yeah, sprite?" He took his duty badge out of his pocket and clipped it to the waistband of his trousers.

"Be careful."

He kissed her. "Always."

He drew his weapon and opened the door just a crack. Hotel staff and party guests lay on the ground the length of the service hallway, terrified expressions on their faces. They seemed to be uninjured. In the distance, he heard a man shouting.

"Everyone, stay down!"

Did the voice belong to security or the shooter?

What he wouldn't give to be in uniform now, not just because he'd be protected by body armor and carrying a lot more firepower, but also because he wouldn't have to waste time proving who he was. Dressed like this, he might be anyone. If he stepped out and security mistook him for another shooter, he'd end up full of holes, and wouldn't that just ruin his fancy shirt?

"Marc!" Sophie said.

He shut the door again. "What is it?"

"I got a text from Holly warning us to get out. She said the shooter was dressed as a server and had an AK."

"Okay. Thanks."

Holding fast to the SIG, he stepped out, heard the door lock behind him.

19:31

REECE STAYED DOWN LIKE the security detail had ordered, his body covering Kara's.

"Lt. Gov. Sheridan, we've secured the rear entrance, and we're taking you and Secretary Holmes out that way."

Reece got to his feet, helped Kara up, her gaze meeting his, her face expressionless apart from the shock in her eyes. Over by the main doors, a member of the security team was draping table linens over the bodies of the two security guards who had stood sentry at the door. Another security guard sat back against the wall, his white shirt covered with blood.

"What about Ambassador DeLacy?"

"He and his team have already left the building."

"And everyone else here? What about the injured?" It felt strange to leave rather than staying to help.

Then again, Reece wanted to get Kara away from this place.

"Ambulances are en route, sir. Most of the hotel guests and staff have already evacuated the building thanks to the fire alarm, but we're locking down the mezzanine level until we're certain the shooter had no accomplices. We don't want wolves escaping because they hid among the sheep."

"Good work."

Secretary Holmes met them at the back door of the ballroom, her mouth a grim line, the faint whiff of cigarette smoke following her. "Will my car be waiting? I don't want to walk around the block in this cold with armed crazies out there."

"Yes, ma'am. The car should be waiting for us."

The three surviving and uninjured security guards closed ranks around them, guiding them out of the ballroom to a service hallway and then toward the exit.

"A man with a gun!" someone shouted.

Everyone gasped and whirled, the security guards pivoting with weapons raised.

Reece turned to see Hunter, arms over his head, weapon in hand.

"I'm a police officer," he shouted, his gaze meeting Reece's for just a moment. "My duty badge is clipped to my waistband."

One of the security guards started toward him.

Reece caught the man by the arm, stopped him. "It's okay. I know him. He's captain of DPD's SWAT team and a friend."

Hunter pointed behind him. "Sophie's in the bathroom. Can you get her out?"

Kara looked up at Reece, and he answered, "Of course."

"Thanks, man." Hunter backed up, opened the door, and a moment later Sophie emerged, Hunter's dinner coat and cummerbund tucked under one arm. She gave his hand a squeeze, then hurried over to Kara.

The two women embraced, but said nothing.

The security guard motioned them forward. "Let's keep moving."

With two security guards in front of them and one following behind, they made their way through a door to a stairway, Kara holding tightly to Reece's hand. No one spoke as they went down two flights of stairs, the blare of the fire alarm echoing in the stairwell.

One of the guards pushed the back door open, cold night air rushing in.

Rat-at-at-at!

Blood sprayed across the door behind the guard, who fell lifeless to the ground.

Screams.

On instinct, Reece grabbed Sophie's hand and drew both Kara and Sophie back toward the stairs, some plan half-formed in his mind about finding safety in the basement. "Secretary Holmes! This way!"

His foot hadn't so much as hit the first step when men in dark green camo rushed up the stairs, rifles pointing straight at Reece.

Heart slamming in his chest, Reece stood his ground, drew Kara and Sophie behind him, some part of him certain they were all about to die.

Then one of the men hitched his rifle over his shoulder and started up the stairs, a grin on his face. "You can't leave our little *rumba* now, Lt. Gov. Sheridan. It is just getting started."

19:37

"GODDAMN IT!" MARC TOOK cover behind a corner pillar, gunfire seeming to come from every direction, including the rear exit. He'd been grazed on his left rib cage, pain making him swear, his shirt torn, blood staining the cloth.

Sophie.

He counted four—no, five—assailants near the top of the stairs, all wearing camo BDUs and armed with military-grade assault rifles, and another fourteen or fifteen down in the lobby. Where the hell had they come from? With the one who lay dead outside the Grand Ballroom, that made for as many as twenty perpetrators.

This wasn't a random shooting. It was a fucking terrorist attack.

Marc was outgunned and outnumbered. If he'd had a rifle or some stun grenades… But he didn't. He had a pistol and six rounds.

From the Grand Ballroom came gunshots and screams.

Marc peered around the pillar, and then he saw her.

Holly! God, no.

She lay unconscious on her back not far from the fire alarm, blood spilling from a head wound.

She'd seen the shooter, sent a text to warn them, then gone for the fire alarm. Had those first shots been intended for her?

Damn it, Holly. Did you have to be a hero again?

Marc's first impulse was to run to her, but there was no way he could reach her without being seen and shot or taken captive. Then the door

Sophie had walked through only moments ago flew open, and five more assailants entered with prisoners.

Sophie!

She and Kara were huddled together, Secretary Holmes walking in front of them, Sheridan in the rear, the barrel of what looked like an HK G36 pressed into his back.

At least they were all alive.

They were all alive.

One of the attackers aimed his weapon at the ceiling and fired, debris raining down on terrified hotel staff. "All of you! On your feet! Get back into the ballroom!"

Men and women lurched to their feet and ran, some sobbing, Marc unable to do a goddamn thing but watch as all of them were forced into the Grand Ballroom.

Son of a bitch!

He'd sent Sophie out that way. And now these bastards—whoever they were—had her. They had all of them—Sheridan, Kara, Secretary Holmes.

And Holly?

He glanced around the pillar. She still hadn't moved.

Jesus.

He felt a pang in his chest when he thought about Nick getting the news, but quashed it. He didn't have time for emotions.

Do your job, Hunter.

He took out his cell, sent a text message to Chief Irving, trying to think of all the most important details.

Counted at least 24 armed perps in woodland camo BDUs. Hostage situation. Secretary Holmes,

Lt. Gov & his wife in hostile hands. Dozens of civilians also captive, incl. my wife. Some injured. Several dead outside the ballroom.

He thought about it for a moment, then sent another message. If it were Sophie, he'd want to know.

Holly Andris is down. Can't get near her. Inform Cobra. They have resources, can perhaps join the fight.

Marc knew the feds would step in now. With the US Secretary of State's safety on the line, they'd send in the HRT—the FBI's Hostage Rescue Team.

Movement down below caught his eye. In the hotel lobby, a several men were busy rigging something to the doors. Explosives.

He sent another text.

Perps are setting charges on main doors.

Four attackers broke off from the main group and headed for the elevators, carrying a heavy case between them.

The elevator closed, moved upward.

And it hit him.

They were headed for the roof. That case probably held some kind of machine gun—or maybe RPGs.

If he didn't reach the roof before they did, they would hold the high ground. And they'd be able to mow down every cop, every paramedic, and every SWAT officer Denver could throw at them.

But how could he make it to the roof?

He glanced around, noticing for the first time the iron grill work that made up the balustrade of each floor of the hotel from the mezzanine to the very top of the atrium. If he'd tried to climb that, he'd be exposed to every shooter in the lobby. Then again, he didn't have to climb all the way to the top, only to the next floor, where he could grab an elevator. With any luck, the assholes were too busy setting booby traps to notice him.

With no other option and the clock ticking, he tucked the pistol into its pocket holster, stepped up onto the railing, and started to climb.

Where the hell was Rossiter when you needed him?

19:40

WHERE THE HELL WAS Hunter?

Gabe watched the bastard with the AK pace back and forth in front of the door, talking in Spanish on his cell phone.

"He's telling them we blocked the door," Joaquin whispered from behind him. "He's saying they have control of the room and everyone in it, but he's asking someone named Pepe what to do now."

The moment the shooting had started, Gabe and Joaquin had run to the doors and closed them, then carried one of the heavy dining tables over to bar them. He'd turned around, started toward the windows, thinking that one of them must open onto a fire escape. Then Kat had shouted for him.

He'd turned to find that two of the servers had assault rifles—and both were pointed at him.

He'd thought they were dealing with a lone shooter.

He'd thought wrong.

He had no idea how many terrorists were in and around the Grand Ballroom. There were two of them in here, and more than a hundred newspaper staff. If Hunter were here, they might be able to come up with a plan and overpower the bastards. As it was, Gabe was the only person in the room with law enforcement experience.

"I'm worried about Holly," Matt whispered. "If she saw them—"

"Hey, *pendejo*. Shut up!" The one who wasn't on the phone glared at Matt. "No talking."

Gabe was worried about Holly, too—and Marc and Sophie, who had disappeared. He hoped the three of them had gotten out. But more than that, he was worried about Kat. This stress couldn't be good for her or the baby. He'd seen terror in her eyes for that brief moment when she'd believed he was about to be shot.

And that's why you're going to sit here and be a good little hostage.

His job was to keep her safe and alive, not to get shot to death in front of her in some half-baked escape attempt, leaving her to raise their kids alone.

He wrapped his arm around her shoulder. "It's going to be okay."

She nodded, but he could feel the tension in her body.

If he'd had his cell phone, he'd have done his best to send Hunter a text, but the sons of bitches had confiscated everyone's phones, along with their wallets, watches, and cash. He had no way of knowing what was happening outside those doors—or who would come through them when they opened.

The one with the phone ended the call and turned toward them. He flagged Gabe and Joaquin with his AK, motioning toward the door. "You. Move the table back."

Gabe gave Kat's hand a squeeze and walked with Joaquin to the table.

"Whatever you have in mind, count me in," Joaquin whispered.

Gabe met his gaze, gave a slight shake of his head to let him know that he had nothing planned. Now wasn't the time.

They'd both taken one end of the table when the guy with the phone moved in on Kat, saying something to her in Spanish, the muzzle of his weapon pointed at the floor.

Gabe almost dropped his end of the table, the impulse to shove that bastard away from her overpowering.

She glared up at the man. "I don't speak Spanish. I'm Diné. Navajo."

"*India Navaja.*" He grinned, pointed to her belly with the muzzle, the sight knotting Gabe's gut. "You've got a baby. Don't worry. We won't hurt you."

Gabe wanted to kill him. He set his end of the table down, walked with Joaquin back to the group, stood face to face with the son of a bitch. He spoke slowly, enunciating every syllable. "Stay away from her."

For a moment he thought the man was going to punch him, his body tensing for a fight. Then the other one opened the doors and started shouting.

"On your feet! Stand up! Move!"

They were herded out into the hallway, around the corner onto the balcony and toward the Great Ballroom.

Gabe took Kat's hand.

A flurry of gasps. A cry.

"Oh, my God!"

There were dead and wounded lying on the floor outside the Grand Ballroom just as he'd feared there would be.

"I hope our photographer is getting photos of this," Baird said.

Gabe put his arm around Kat's shoulder, drew her close. "Look at me."

He would do what he could for the wounded—if they'd let him—once he felt certain Kat was safe.

From a few feet in front of him, he heard Matt. "Holly! God, no!"

Joaquin pushed past Gabe, cursing in Spanish.

There on the floor lay Holly, and it looked like she'd taken a round to the head.

"Jesus!" Gabe started toward her, Kat standing rooted to the spot, wide-eyed, hand over her mouth.

"Get back!" one of their captors shouted, pointing his rifle at Matt and Joaquin, who had almost reached Holly's side.

Joaquin shouted something in Spanish, kept moving toward her.

Matt was right beside him. "She's my friend. I'm going to help her, and you're going to have to shoot me to stop me."

Gabe raised his hands over his head. "I'm a paramedic. I can help her."

Joaquin quickly translated. "*Es un paramédico.*"

The three of them knelt down beside her, and Gabe saw that she was breathing. He felt for a pulse, found it strong and steady. "She's alive. It looks like a graze. She might have a concussion or even a skull fracture."

Damn it!

He didn't have the equipment to deal with this.

One of the assholes started shouting again, motioning for them to go into the ballroom. But Gabe wouldn't leave her here no matter what they aimed at him.

"Matt, you carry her legs. Joaquin, carry her upper body, and try to keep it stable. I'm going to support her head and neck with my hands. Lift on three. One. Two. Three."

Slowly, carefully, they carried Holly into the ballroom.

CHAPTER FOUR

19:40

Marc stopped, fought to catch his breath, pressing a hand against the pain in his ribs. His fingers came away bloody. There was nothing he could do about that now. He had bigger problems. He could just hear the bad guys talking to one another somewhere on the roof above. He wouldn't be able to sneak up on them breathing like he'd just run up seven flights of stairs.

That's why they call it FAT Tire, Hunter.

Yeah, too much beer—and too little time in the gym.

He'd ditched the idea of taking an elevator when the doors had opened with a loud *ding* that had made every asshole in the lobby look up. He'd had to take off his dress shoes because the soles made so much noise, every step echoing in the stairwell. Now he was running around with a pistol in his hand and wearing nothing but socks, tuxedo pants, a starched white shirt stained red with his own blood—and a fine black tie.

Just like James fucking Bond.

His heartbeat and respiration slowed, Sophie's lingering scent reminding him with every breath exactly what was at stake tonight. He did his best to put her out of his mind. He wouldn't be able to help her or anyone else if he didn't focus.

Sheridan will keep her safe. She'll be okay.

So, what now?

He leaned back against the cold concrete wall, mulled over the possibilities.

There were four of them, and he had four bullets left. Even if he snuck up on them, he doubted he'd be able to squeeze off four rounds with absolute accuracy using only a pistol before one of them lit him up. What he needed was a way to eliminate all four of them at once without giving himself away.

Dream on, buddy.

He slowly climbed the last flight of stairs, stopping to the left of the open door, frigid night air pouring in from the darkness. He glanced around the corner.

Nothing.

He stepped outside. It wasn't as dark as he'd thought it would be, security lights on the parapets casting an eerie yellow glow. He glanced around, pistol raised, finger on the trigger. The hotel's triangular roof was a maze of external ductwork, enormous ventilation and air conditioning units, what looked like a greenhouse and...

Beehives?

Keeping low, he made his way around the bulkhead and along a long line of ductwork, aware that his white shirt made him highly visible in the darkness. A movement. Voices.

He froze.

All four of them were gathered at the south end of the building, near its prow where the Palace overlooked the star-shaped intersection of

Broadway, Seventeenth, and Court Place, with its public park and bus stops. They were bent over something with flashlights. One of them moved, giving Marc a quick view.

A Ma Deuce.

The bastards had a fucking Ma Deuce—a Browning M2 machine gun. If they managed to get that thing up and running, they would have enough firepower to take down targets up to two thousand yards away.

Marc's SWAT team would be fish in a barrel.

He took a moment to think, trying to ignore the fact that he was fucking freezing, the frigid wind cutting right through him. He made his way back along the ductwork to a place he felt was secure, and then pulled out his cell phone to send Irving a text.

Four perps on roof setting up a Browning M2 .50 cal. May have RPGs, etc. I'm going to try to take them out.

If he failed, at least Irving and Marc's team would be warned.

Quickly and quietly, he retraced his path along the ductwork, moving in closer this time, trying to make up for the limited range of his pistol. He tried to line up a shot, felt himself shivering.

Get a grip, Hunter!

He willed his body to relax, surrendered to the cold, then set it out of his mind.

He lined up his shot and ... squeezed the trigger.

Bam!

One down.

Shouting at one another, the others grabbed their weapons, one aiming into the darkness and spraying bullets in Marc's general direction, rounds slamming into the ductwork around him with a dull *thwack thwack thwack thwack thwack*.

Bent low, he ran, taking cover behind some AC vents and peering out at the three men, ignoring the vibration of his cell phone. Two perps had gone back to work on the M2, while the third stood sentry, rifle over his shoulder, cell phone in his hand, thumb moving over the screen. He was probably calling for backup.

Well, Marc couldn't let him get away with that. He took aim, fired again.

Bam!

Another one down.

The others had laid their weapons aside to work on the Ma Deuce.

Marc saw his chance.

He rushed them, stopping to fire at the first one to aim a rifle at him.

Bam!

A miss.

Shit!

Fueled by a surge of adrenaline, Marc dove for cover.

19:45

TESSA DARCANGELO TURNED THE lights down low and snuggled against her husband, Julian, the sight of four sleeping children and the twinkling Christmas tree making her smile. Chase had crashed on the recliner, a Lego thingy of his own creation clutched in his hand. Maire lay next to the tree. Addy had fallen asleep with her face in her Santa coloring book. Little Tristan was curled up on the dog bed with his blankie and Shadow, their nine-month-old German shepherd puppy.

"At last," she said. "Silence."

Julian chuckled, his fingers threading through hers, his lips brushing her cheek. "Think we can slip away for a little adult playtime?"

She laughed. "Marc and Sophie will be here soon."

They were watching Chase and Addy tonight so that Marc and Sophie could go to the newspaper's holiday party. It had been a happy kind of chaos, the house taken over by four kids ages seven and under. Together, she and Julian had managed to feed them all, keep them entertained, and prevent them from hurting themselves or each other. It felt like an accomplishment.

She smiled, an image of Julian giving the kids reindeer rides on his back flashing through her mind. "You know what I love about you?"

"Yeah, I do. It sits about four inches below my navel."

She laughed, gave his ribs a nudge with her elbow. "I love how sweet you are with children. I would never have imagined that the big, bad FBI agent I met all those years ago would be a teddy bear with little kids."

He kissed her hair. "Anything good in me comes from loving you."

She knew that wasn't true, but she didn't say so. She snuggled into the hard wall of his chest, allowed herself to relax and savor the moment. Neither she nor Julian had had Christmases like this as children. But together, they were discovering new joys, giving their kids the things they'd never had.

Julian's work phone rang.

"Shit." Julian kissed her again. "I've got to get this."

He leaned forward, grabbed his phone from the coffee table. "Darcangelo."

He stood, his expression turning dark. "Son of a bitch! How long ago?"

Tessa's pulse skipped. She stood and followed Julian toward their bedroom, his questions and the tension on his face leaving no doubt.

Something terrible had happened.

He opened the closet, tossed his night BDUs onto the bed. "Do they know how many? Did they get out? Damn it! I'm on my way. Yeah, I'll meet you there."

"What is it? What happened?"

He stripped off his jeans and shirt, his blue eyes hard. "Terrorists attacked the Palace Hotel. Everyone who didn't get out has been taken hostage."

"What?" Tessa's heart gave a hard knock, breath rushing from her lungs. "That's where the I-Team party is."

Julian tied his dark hair back in a short ponytail, and then yanked a black turtleneck over his head. "The British Consulate General was also having its Christmas party tonight. Cops on the ground say the British ambassador got away, but the bastards caught the Secretary of State and her entourage at the back exit. Reece, Kara, and Sophie were with her."

"Oh, no." Tessa sank onto the bed. "What about the others?"

A muscle clenched in his jaw. "Hunter broke away. He was feeding intel to Irving for a while. He told the old man that a group of combatants was setting up an M2—that's a heavy machine gun—on the roof and that he was going to try to stop them. Irving has tried reaching him but hasn't heard back since."

Dear God.

Marc was Julian's best friend. He and Sophie and Reece and Kara were like family. If anything happened to him, to any of them …

"And the others?"

Julian stepped into his pants, yanked up the zipper, reached for his shirt. "Hunter told Irving Holly was down. He didn't know whether she was still alive or …"

"Sweet Jesus." Tessa's stomach knotted. "Does Nick know?"

The two were just shy of their first wedding anniversary.

"Irving didn't say." Julian pulled the T-shirt over his head.

"Who would do this?"

"We don't know—yet. But we're going to find out, and they're going to pay."

For a moment, neither of them spoke, Julian stepping into his black boots and lacing them. He unlocked the gun safe in the back of their closet, took out a pistol and slipped it into his shoulder holster, then grabbed his rifle case and his gear bag. "I probably won't be home tonight. Don't wait up."

"You think I could sleep with all of you in danger?" She followed him to the front door. "Has Megan heard?"

Megan was Marc's younger sister. She and her husband, Nate West, lived up at the Cimarron—the West family's mountain ranch.

"I don't know. Call her. I'm sure she'd rather hear it from us." He leaned down, pressed a kiss to her lips. "I love you."

"I love you, too. Please come home in one piece."

"I'll do my best."

Tessa watched him climb into his pickup and drive away, fear for him mingling with fear for her friends. She'd thought she'd get used to being a cop's wife, but there was nothing easy about knowing her husband was going into danger. She'd come close to losing him more than once already.

Feeling almost sick, she walked into the living room, her gaze falling on Chase and Addy, their innocence making her heart constrict. They had no idea their parents were in mortal danger.

One by one, she carried the kids to bed, putting Chase and Addy in the big bed in the guestroom. Then, feeling wooden, she walked into the kitchen, picked up the phone, and called the Cimarron.

19:50

"ARE YOU READY TO PUT the star on top, Miss Emily?"

"Yes!"

Megan West sat on the sofa beside her husband, Nate, who bounced little Jackson on his lap, both of them watching while Grandpa Jack handed their daughter the family's heirloom gold-plated star and lifted her onto his shoulders.

"Let's put the star on top your head," Emily teased, doing just that.

"Do I look like a Christmas tree to you? What are they teaching kids in school these days?"

Emily laughed.

Jack walked up to the tree, Emily sitting on his shoulders. "Reach out as far as you can—just like that. Now settle the star on that branch on top that's sticking straight up. Do you see it?"

"Uh-huh." Emily settled the star into place.

"Look at that." Jack grinned. "The kid's a natural. You'd think she's been putting stars on top of Christmas trees all her life."

Emily beamed at the praise, turned to Megan and Nate. "Did you see, Mommy? Did you see, Daddy?"

Nate chuckled. "I sure did."

Megan nodded. "Great job, sweetie."

"Hurray!" Janet cheered, dandling chubby Lily on her lap.

Born three weeks apart last summer, Jackson and Lily were six months old and about to celebrate their first Christmas.

"Now can we turn on the lights?"

Jack knelt down, picked up the switch that controlled the tree. "What do you say we let Janet do the honors?"

Emily nodded, took the switch, and carried it to Janet as if she were giving Janet a bouquet of flowers.

Janet accepted it just as graciously. "Thank you. Do you want to help me?"

Emily smiled and nodded.

It put a bittersweet ache in Megan's chest to see her daughter so loved and so happy. At that age, Megan had been afraid of everyone and everything, weighed down by the constant criticism of her strict adoptive parents. It still amazed her that she was married to Nate, that the Cimarron was her home, that her children would grow up here in comfort and plenty, unburdened by the kind of hardship and uncertainty that she and Marc had known as children.

Nate stood, Jackson still in his arms. "Let me turn out the lights first."

The room went dark, and then...

"Oh!" They all let out a collective sigh.

It was a beautiful tree, decorated with the family's ornaments, from beautiful antiques passed down through three generations to simple decorations made by Nate when he'd been a little boy and now by Emily, too.

Megan looked over at Jackson, found him looking wide-eyed at the tree, and felt a lump in her throat. "What do you think, pumpkin? It's your first Christmas tree."

"Do we get hot chocolick now, Grandpa Jack?" Emily asked.

"You bet." Jack headed for the kitchen. "On a special night like tonight, a body's got to have hot chocolick."

Megan and Nate shared a smile. One day someone was going to have to ruin Jack's fun and teach the girl that it was choco-*late*. But not tonight.

"With marshmallows?"

"You want fifty or a hundred marshmallows?"

"A hundred!"

"Ten marshmallows, old man," Nate called after them, handing Megan the baby and walking to the fireplace to toss on another log. "He is spoiling her."

The phone rang.

"I got it," Jack called from the kitchen. "And I heard that."

A moment later, he reappeared, the expression on his face filling Megan's stomach with dread, sending adrenaline through her veins.

"It's Tessa Darcangelo." He reached for Jackson. "You two might want to take this call in my study."

Dear God, what had happened?

19:50

IT WAS DOWN TO one now.

Marc was out of ammo and chilled to the bone, his fingers and toes hurting with cold. He needed to end this and get indoors before he became hypothermic. But this last bastard was proving difficult to kill, keeping to the shadows, moving from place to place like a ghost. Marc wondered if he had some kind of night-vision gear. He hadn't noticed anyone wearing NVGs, but then he'd had barely more than a glance at any of these assholes. The guy could have been carrying something. Then again, Marc's shirt all but glowed in the dark. The bastard probably didn't need NVGs to see him.

Keeping low, Marc circled back toward the perpetrator's original position at the prow of the building. He could see the M2 and a case with some other gear in it. He could also see the bodies of the first two men he'd dropped. But there was every chance that his target was watching this position, waiting for Marc to expose himself in his quest for a weapon and more ammo.

If the situation had been different, Marc would simply have played a waiting game. His years as a Special Forces sniper had taught him patience. But if he stayed out here much longer, he'd be in trouble.

He found himself looking at the camo jackets on the two dead bodies and the rifles they'd dropped as they fell. And an idea came to him.

He quickly stripped out of his white shirt and crept on his belly toward the nearer of the two corpses, the wind bitter cold against his bare skin. He took the man's rifle, checked it, then set it aside. Then he removed the man's jacket and put it on himself. It was too small and wet with blood, but who gave a shit? It was warmer than what he'd been wearing.

Next, he took his shirt and put it on the dead man. Not bothering to button all the buttons, he dragged the body toward the parapet and propped it in a sitting position, his white shirt like a beacon in the darkness.

He quickly backed away and lay down where the corpse had been, rifle in hand, finger on the trigger. And there he waited.

But not for long.

An explosion of gunfire.

Out of the corner of his eye, he saw three new holes appear in his white shirt.

He slowed his breathing, held deathly still.

Footsteps.

Another burst of gunfire, this time from nearby.

His quarry stepped out of the darkness, cursing, and made straight for the dead body he believed was Marc, his boots passing within inches of Marc's face.

In one motion, Marc rolled onto his back, raised the rifle, and fired.

Rat-at-at-at!

The son of a bitch jerked around, stared at him in stunned surprise, then toppled backward off the building.

Marc stood, strode to the edge, watched as the bastard fell eight stories to the ground. "Thanks for choosing the Palace Hotel. We hope you enjoyed our service."

He searched the other bodies, confiscating wallets, IDs, and cell phones. He yanked a camo-style ball cap off one and put it on his head, hoping it would help conceal his face from the security cameras inside the hotel. These bastards probably had control of the security room by now, and that meant they were in a position to watch the stairs, hallways, and elevators.

Then he hurried back to the M2, saw that they had very nearly assembled it. A half-dozen belts of .50-cal ammo lay beside it. They also had a Russian RPG-7 that could take out a tank, as well as—*holy shit!*—a McMillan TAC-338 sniper rifle with a fucking scope and plenty of ammo.

"Oh, you beautiful baby! Come to Daddy."

It really *was* Christmas.

The sniper rifle he would put to good use, but what about the rest of this shit? He couldn't leave it here, or the bad guys might get their hands on it again, and he couldn't stay out here and babysit it.

He dialed Irving's number. "The roof is ours. But, hey, we have a situation."

CHAPTER FIVE

19:50

Kat rubbed the ache in her back, watching from across the room while Gabe did what he could to help a man who'd been shot in the abdomen.

"We can save his life, but he needs to go to a hospital," he explained to one of their captors, his blood-stained hands holding compress of napkins against the wound in the man's belly. "I know you can understand me. He needs attention *now*!"

Some part of her worried that Gabe would push their captors too far. These men had no respect for life. No, they weren't men. They were soulless monsters wearing the skins of men. Trying to appeal to their sense of decency and compassion might get Gabe killed. But she knew it was impossible for him to witness human suffering and not do everything he could to help.

Gabe had a reverence for all life. That's why he was a paramedic. That's why he'd been a park ranger. That's why she loved him. She wouldn't change that about him, even to keep him safe. And yet she couldn't shake the sense of urgency.

They needed to get out of here—now.

Reece stood as close to Gabe as the bastards with the guns would allow. "Do you want more people to die? Show some compassion, for God's sake. Let paramedics take the wounded."

Nearby, Sophie and Joaquin were following Gabe's instructions, cleaning the blood from Holly's hair, while Matt sat on the floor beside her, speaking to her and holding her hand.

"I came to this party with you, and I'm not leaving without you."

Holly moaned but didn't open her eyes.

"The bullet made an inch-long track, split her scalp." Joaquin was bent over her, looking at the wound on the side of her head. "There's a big bruise, but the bleeding has stopped."

Sophie took the handkerchief from Matt's dinner jacket and handed it to Kat. "Can you fill this with ice from the bar or something? And bring more napkins."

Sophie wasn't just worried about Holly or their situation, Kat knew. She was also worried about Marc. No one had seen him since he'd sent Sophie off with Reece.

"I'll see what I can find." Kat walked toward one of the serving tables, rubbing her back, the movement helping to take away some of the pain.

One of the monsters stepped into her path. "Get back over there."

Kat willed herself to look him in the eyes, felt anger instead of fear. "My friend is hurt. We need ice and paper towels or napkins to help with the swelling and bleeding. If you won't let me get them, then you'll have to get them for us."

His gaze dropped to her belly before he motioned her on with a jerk of his head.

She found a stack of cocktail napkins on one end of the buffet table, grabbed a handful, along with another bottle of water just in case. Then she took a handful of ice from the container that held the water bottles and tied it into the handkerchief.

"How is Holly?"

Kat turned to see Kara standing a few feet away from her, two bottled waters in her hands. "She's still unconscious. It looks like a bullet grazed—"

"No talking! You!" One of the bastards grabbed Kara by the arm, jerked her away from Kat. "Get back over there."

Their kidnappers had forced Secretary Holmes to sit by herself at a table near the center of the room, then divided the rest of them into three groups—newspaper employees, those who'd attended the British ambassador's party, and hotel staff and other workers. They were still looking through people's IDs, calling people aside when they had questions about what they did for a living or why they'd come to the hotel tonight. Kat didn't understand why it was so important to them that the three groups remain separated, but it left her feeling afraid.

Their captors seemed to have a plan, but only they knew what it was.

Why were they doing this?

She carried the supplies back to Sophie. "I hope this is enough."

"Thanks." Sophie frowned. "Are you okay?"

"My back aches from all this standing."

"I'll get you a chair," Tom said.

As he turned to walk away, five more armed men entered the room. They were dressed the same as the others, except for the one in front, who wore a red beret. From the way he carried himself—and the way he barked out commands to the others—she could tell he was the one in charge.

He walked over to Secretary Holmes, a sneer on his face, then glanced around at the rest of them. "Quiet! *¡Cállense!*"

One of his men fired shots into the ceiling, making Kat jump.

Apart from the moans of the wounded, the room fell silent.

Reece stepped forward. "Who the hell are you? Six people are dead. Ten more are wounded. I want to know why."

Fear for Reece made Kat's pulse spike, the ache in her back growing sharp.

Then she felt something trickling down her leg.

She looked down, saw the trickle become a gush.

Sophie saw. "Oh, God. Your water."

Kat stared down, her heart tripping. "I'm … I'm not due for five more weeks."

She couldn't be in labor—not now, not here.

19:50

ZACH MCBRIDE KISSED HIS way up his wife's body, lingering on her faint silver stretch marks, her taste still alive on his tongue, her scent filling his head, fueling his lust.

"Don't." Natalie's fingers were still fisted in his hair, and she used them to lift his mouth away from her skin.

"Why not?" He pressed his lips to her belly again.

"You can't seriously find stretch marks sexy."

As horny as he was, it took a moment for him to shift gears. He'd known she felt self-conscious about the changes pregnancy had made to her body, but he hadn't realized it bothered her this much. She ought to be basking in the post-orgasmic glow, not feeling ashamed because carrying an eight-pound human being inside her had left its mark.

Or maybe your oral sex skills aren't quite what you think they are.

"What if I *do* find them sexy?"

She gave a little laugh. "That's sweet of you to say, but—"

"No, I mean it." Shit. How could he explain this? She was the writer in the family, not he. "When I see your stretch marks, I think of how good it feels to come deep inside you. I think of us making a baby together. I think of everything you went through to bring Aiden into the world—morning sickness, swollen ankles, eighteen hours of labor. These changes in your body tell a story, and I'm at the heart of that story. I'm the cause. God, Natalie, don't you get it? Those little silver lines tell me you love me—and *that* turns me on."

He didn't wait for her response, but kissed her slow and deep, his hand moving to caress her breasts, his thumb teasing a puckered nipple. "Those ten extra pounds you can't seem to lose? They're all in the right places. Your breasts are fuller, your hips and ass are a little rounder. Can't you feel how much you turn me on?"

He nudged her hip with his erection, then lowered his head, drew a nipple into his mouth, and sucked, reaching down between her thighs to stroke her. She was so incredibly wet—the result of his mouth and her climax.

She moaned, arched into his hand, spread her thighs wide, her fingers gripping his cock, tugging him, telling him where she wanted him to be.

Somewhere in the background, his cell phone rang again.

He ignored it.

He settled himself between her parted thighs and sank into her, their moans mingling as he filled her, then withdrew and thrust again. "When I see those stretch marks, angel, I think of *this*."

Her eyes were shut, her lips parted, her dark hair fanned against her pillow, breath leaving her in little moans. How could she imagine for a moment that she was somehow less attractive to him? He loved her body, worshiped it, was amazed by it.

"*Natalie.*" He leaned down, pressed his lips against her pulse.

She wrapped her legs around his waist, her nails digging into the muscles of his bare ass, urging him to go faster, harder. He was only too happy to oblige. He was on fire for her, every inch of him burning with need, his cock slick with her wetness. But he didn't want to come, not yet, not before she'd come again.

He thrust hard, buried himself deep inside her, then ground his pubic bone against hers, putting pressure where she needed it most. Her moans turned to whimpers, a pink flush stealing over her breasts as it always did just before she came. Then she cried out his name, her inner muscles clenching around him.

God, yes.

He picked up where he'd left off, driving into her fast and hard, wanting ... craving ... needing. "*Natalie.*"

Orgasm hit him with the force of a blast wave, pleasure scorching through him, leaving him spent, his mind empty, his heart full.

Afterward, they held each other, her head on his chest, their legs tangled beneath the sheets. They'd both begun to doze off when his cell phone rang *again*.

"Shit." He kissed her hair, scooted out of the bed, then shuffled into the kitchen, buck naked. "McBride."

"Where the hell have you been?" It was Teresa Rowan, U.S. Marshal for the Colorado territory—his boss.

He figured it was best not to answer with the truth. "I was asleep. What's up?"

"Terrorists have taken over the Palace Hotel. There are casualties. I don't know how many are dead, but the bastards have more than three hundred hostages, including the Secretary of State and your buddies Lt. Gov. Sheridan and Marc Hunter."

"*Jesus.*" He turned back toward the bedroom.

"The FBI Hostage Rescue Team is taking the lead on this one, but they haven't arrived yet. Denver's SWAT team is on the scene, along with FBI SWAT. I thought you'd want to be there, too."

"I sure as hell do."

"They've set up an incident command center at United Nations Park a couple of blocks south of the hotel."

"I'm on my way."

He found Natalie sitting up in bed. "What's wrong? What is it?"

He picked up the TV remote and turned to CNN, then started getting dressed. "Terrorists have taken over the Palace Hotel and have taken hostages. The Secretary of State is among them. So are Sheridan and Hunter. They have reports that some people have been killed, but there aren't any details."

Natalie stared at the screen wide-eyed. "Everyone is there—most of our friends. Tonight was the I-Team holiday party. Oh, God!"

19:51

PEPE LOOKED AT SHERIDAN'S arrogant face and wanted to cut him to pieces, to make an example of him for the others so that no one would dare talk to him like that. The *cabrón* still thought he was giving the orders. But he was wrong.

Pendejo de mierda.

But Pepe needed the man, so killing him now was not an option, even as an example to the others. But he didn't need the bastard's wife.

Before Sheridan could react, Pepe backhanded her, almost knocking her to the floor, his knuckles splitting her cheek.

Gasps. A cry. Silence.

Sheridan caught his wife, held her, hatred unmistakable in his eyes when his gaze again met Pepe's.

"Next time you speak to me without respect, I'll turn her over to my men."

The hatred in Sheridan's eyes grew sharper.

Happy with the way his striking the bitch had gotten everyone's attention, Pepe looked around him, then spoke to their most honored guest. "Madam Secretary, I am Commander Moreno of La Fuerza de Liberación de Colombia. You arranged for my cousin's abduction from Colombia, but tonight you're going to make up for that. If you do as I say, no one else will die." Not right now, anyway. He needed them as leverage. "There is plenty of food, thanks to the British ambassador, who, sadly, managed to run away from our little party. So relax and enjoy the food and wine."

The bitch glared at him, dried blood on her cheek. "The US government doesn't negotiate with terrorists."

"Let us hope you are wrong—for your sake." He glanced around at the others. "The rest of you, keep your mouths shut, and do as you are told."

"What about the wounded?" asked a man Pepe hadn't noticed before. He knelt beside a guy who'd been shot in the gut, his hands pressed against the man's belly. "I'm a paramedic. We can save this man's life if we get him to a hospital."

Pepe didn't give a damn about saving lives. As far as he was concerned, everyone in this room was already dead. But these American men were soft.

"If you let the wounded and the women go, it would be taken as a sign of good faith," Sheridan said, his tone less haughty, his eyes still blazing, his wife behind him, beyond Pepe's reach.

Of course the *malparido* would want the women to go free. He wanted to protect his whore of a wife. But Pepe wasn't that stupid. The women were the key to controlling the men. Besides, he'd already made up his mind about who would go free and who would stay, who would live and who would die.

"Juandi, see to it that the wounded and the dead are taken down to the loading dock. Watch for cops pretending to be EMTs." Then he turned to the hotel staff, many of whom were Latinos, and switched to Spanish. "*Ustedes son libres de irse también. La lucha de la FLC no es con la clase obrera.*"

You are free to go as well. The FLC has no fight with the working class.

Disbelief showed on their faces. They looked at one another, some translating for those who hadn't understood, none of them brave enough to walk past him out the door.

The sheep always needed a shepherd.

He turned to Jhon, still speaking in Spanish. "Show them to the loading dock. Make sure they get out safely." He pointed to the paramedic, switched back to English. "You help them get the wounded out, then find someone to help you carry the dead."

The paramedic looked boldly up at him. "I'm not leaving without my wife."

Pepe didn't like this man any more than he did Sheridan. The whoreson was far too bold, too impertinent. "Who is your wife?"

The paramedic met his gaze but said nothing, too clever to answer.

Pepe turned to his men, switched back to Spanish. "You three help Juandi. Make sure this *malparido gonorrea* leaves with the wounded. If he refuses, shoot him."

His cell phone buzzed. It was the text he'd been waiting for.

El regalo de Navidad en el sótano está listo.

The little Christmas present they'd been assembling in the basement was ready.

Tavo appeared at his side. "We're almost done checking the rooms. Most of the guests escaped because of the fire alarm."

Pepe acknowledged him with a nod, his body revved on adrenaline.

Why hadn't he heard from Luis? The last text he'd gotten from the *pendejo* said he was having trouble putting the machine gun together in the dark. Pepe shouted to Camilo to head up to the roof to help him, then took out the mobile phone he'd prepared for this special moment and dialed 911, speaking clearly and slowly.

"This is Commander Moreno of La Fuerza de Liberación de Colombia. I have taken control of the Palace Hotel. Put your chief of police on the line."

19:55

HOLLY OPENED HER EYES, found herself looking up at Joaquin.

"How do you feel?"

Why was he whispering?

Someone was holding her hand. Matt?

Sophie was there, too, looking down at her, worry in her eyes.

"What—?"

Joaquin pressed a finger to her lips. "Shh. The hotel has been taken over by terrorists. We're all hostages. These crazy motherfuckers killed six people. An AK round grazed your head, knocked you out."

Bits and pieces of it came back to her. The server with the AK. Her calls to Nick and 911. The guards. The fire alarm. And now a rotten headache.

Freaking perfect.

She tried to sit, but Joaquin held her down.

"They're letting the wounded go. Stay still, and we'll get you out of here." He slowly rose to his feet, then said something in Spanish.

Her friends moved aside as a man dressed in woodland camo pressed in. He looked down at her, then turned and spoke over his shoulder to someone else.

Joaquin responded, again in Spanish, an urgent tone to his voice.

The man in the camo shouted something at Joaquin, then walked away.

Joaquin knelt down, his dark eyes filled with rage, lowered his voice to a whisper. "They won't let you go. One of them said he saw you pull the fire alarm."

"Oh, that," she whispered back.

She pushed aside the knot of fear that had formed in her stomach, ignored the despair. Yes, she wanted to see Nick again, to feel his arms around her, to apologize for her part of their argument. At the same time, she couldn't let herself be taken to safety, not while her friends remained in danger. None of them had her training. She would rather be here doing whatever she could to get them all safely home again than watching it unfold on TV, powerless to help.

She sat up, wincing at the pain in her head, dizziness making her nauseated. "Why are you all still here? Didn't you get my text message?"

"Take this." Sophie pressed a handkerchief filled with ice into her hands. "I didn't see your text until after the shooting had already started."

And Holly remembered that Sophie and Marc had been ... *busy*.

Holly held it to her head. "Who are they?"

"The FLC—Fuerza de Liberación de Colombia," Joaquin whispered. "The Colombian Liberation Force."

Dear God.

Adrenaline shot through her, making her pulse spike.

There'd been no need for Joaquin to translate. She knew about the FLC. They had nothing to do with liberation and everything to do with cocaine smuggling, kidnapping, and murder, using guerilla tactics against those in the Colombian government who couldn't be bought. Their leader, who called himself La Culebra, The Viper, was a sociopath, known for being ruthless. Rumor had it that he'd gotten his nom-de-guerre by tossing his victims to vipers and then watching as they died slow, excruciating deaths. If he was behind this…

Oh, Nick.

The FBI Hostage Rescue Team would have to bring their best game to this fight, or she would never see him again.

CHAPTER SIX

19:59

Nick stood inside the FBI mobile command center, Tower, McBride, and Darcangelo beside him, listening while Chief Irving played back the recording he'd made of that son of a bitch Moreno.

"The US failed to stand by its agreement, so we are taking back what's ours. The Secretary of State will order the release of my cousin, Oscar Moreno Ortíz, from your Supermax. You will bring him to me safely here at the hotel by helicopter before midnight, together with the thirty-five million dollars you stole from us. When he is in the air and on his way, have him call me at this number. I'll tell you what to do next. If you do exactly as I say, no one else will die. If you try to rescue the prisoners, I will kill every last one. If my cousin is not free by midnight, I will execute one prisoner every five minutes until they are all dead."

Chief Irving paused the playback. "That gives us four hours."

Special Agent Dixon, the commander of Denver's FBI SWAT team, motioned for Irving to continue the playback.

"As a gesture of what you call 'good faith,' I will release some of the prisoners, along with the wounded and the bodies of the dead. Their families will want them back. It is almost Christmas, after all. I will allow ambulances to come to the loading dock in ten minutes."

The bastard's tone of voice was smug, so very arrogant, his words sending shards of fear through Nick.

Hunter had told Irving Holly was down. Was she badly hurt? Was she dead?

No. No, she couldn't be.

"Though the US government did not keep its promise to my cousin, I will keep my promise to you," Moreno said.

The recording ended.

"If he keeps his word, he'll start releasing the wounded in five minutes," Irving said. "I asked for volunteers. We've got a dozen ambulances on standby around the corner from the hotel."

"I volunteer to go in with the ambulance crews," Nick said.

Irving shook his head. "I know you're worried about your wife, but the EMTs don't want any LEOs going in with them. They're concerned that a law-enforcement presence might spark a firefight."

Nick bit back words he knew he'd regret.

"If she's wounded, we'll soon know," McBride said softly behind him.

Dixon looked over to a man in a suit. "Who is this Moreno son of a bitch, and what the fuck is he talking about?"

The suit held out a file. "Moreno is the nephew of Oscar Duarte Moreno, known as El Culebra, the elusive head of the FLC, a paramilitary drug cartel. Five years ago, his older son, also named Oscar, murdered a DEA agent and his wife in cold blood. Three years later, the son was taken in a joint, top-secret op between the Colombian special forces, CIA, and DEA that was orchestrated by the State Department."

That's why they'd gone after Secretary Holmes. She'd been the one to authorize the op that had landed little Oscar's ass in prison.

The man in the suit went on. "Oscar Junior was brought to the US, where he cut a deal with prosecutors—a single charge of second-degree murder and a ten-year sentence in exchange for intel that would bring his father's operation down. The kid wouldn't give evidence that DEA investigators found useful, so the judge threw out the deal. The son was tried, convicted, and sentenced to two life terms. He's serving his sentence at ADX here in Florence, Colorado. The State Department seized all of his family's US assets."

"So his cousin is here to spring him and retrieve the money," Dixon said, stating the obvious.

"That's what it sounds like."

"There's more you need to know." Chief Irving took a swig of coffee. "My SWAT captain is on the inside. He and his wife were attending the newspaper's Christmas party. Somehow, he got away, but she's still a hostage. He's been sending me intel via text. He reported at least twenty-four combatants, all wearing woodland camo. He saw some of them heading up to the hotel's rooftop with what he thought might be heavy weapons. He took out four men on the roof who were trying to put together a Browning M2. We hold the high ground."

Nick gave a low whistle.

"Holy shit," McBride muttered.

"Way to go, Hunter," Darcangelo said.

"He's still up there, freezing his ass off in a tux, trying to keep them from retaking the position. He was grazed by a round but says he's okay. He has requested we send a helo to haul away the weapons so they don't fall into enemy hands again. He also has wallets and four cell phones from the assholes he took out."

They'd better give Hunter a medal when this was over. Those cell phones held a wealth of intel that might make the difference for all of them. If they could use them to tap Moreno's phone...

Dixon shook his head. "We can't risk landing a helo up there. Moreno would hear it, interpret it as a rescue action, and start killing people. We—
"

Nick cut him off. "CIS has a specially outfitted Little Bird in our Centennial Airport hangar that we can put at your disposal."

Smaller than a regular helicopter and fitted with special stealth features, the Little Bird could do the job without Moreno hearing a thing.

Dixon's eyes narrowed. "Who are you?"

"Nick Andris, a paramilitary operator with Cobra International Solutions."

"His wife is among the hostages," McBride added. "We got a report from Hunter that she was down. He didn't know whether she was alive or..."

Dead.

The unspoken word tore at Nick's chest.

Dixon shook his head. "I can't send you up there, not even in a Little Bird. We'd be risking too much. Irving, you need to text your SWAT captain and tell him to lie low until this is over. His actions, though laudable, could cause us a world of trouble. How is Moreno going to react when he finds out his men on the roof are dead? If he thinks we're responsible for that, he might kill Secretary Holmes."

Nick couldn't believe what he was hearing.

Darcangelo stepped forward, fury on his face. "You're just going to abandon Hunter? If they find him, they'll kill him. What about the M2? What about the cell phones? He risked his life—"

"We'll ask him to field strip the M2 and hide the parts," Dixon said. "There are a lot of lives at stake here, detective. What Hunter did was courageous, but his actions could imperil this entire operation. In the meantime, you Cobra boys need to leave. Cobra has a great reputation, but you're not going to be a part of this. This is an HRT operation—"

Nick exploded. "Your HRT hasn't gotten here yet!"

"—and we're operating by the book. I don't have to remind you that the Secretary of State is being held at gunpoint, along with your lieutenant governor. You need to step back and sit this out."

"I can't do that, *sir*."

Dixon's gaze went cold. "Anyone who's not federal or Denver PD needs to leave this command vehicle now. I'll allow you to stay here at the incident command center, but you're not going to be a part of our briefings or operation."

"I wouldn't be too sure about that." Tower pulled out his cell phone.

"Don't make me bring in muscle to remove the two of you."

Nick met Tower's gaze, saw that Tower was thinking exactly what he was thinking.

"I'll keep you up to date," McBride said. "You go and talk to the ambulance crews, show them Holly's photo, give them your cell number."

"Thanks." Nick turned to go, his hands clenched into fists.

Tower started after him, then stopped. "I ran an op against the FLC once a few years ago. Moreno is every bit as ruthless as his uncle. I seriously doubt he intends to let the hostages go. He'll want to exact revenge for his family's loss of face. You need to find out what this bastard's real endgame is, or people are going to die."

20:05

GABE RETURNED TO THE Grand Ballroom, the wounded all loaded into ambulances, apart from Holly, who apparently wasn't going anywhere. His job now was to carry the dead. "I'm going to need some help," he said. "Any volunteers?"

Ramirez was on his feet. "I'll help."

"Count me in," said Alex Carmichael.

"I'll help too," Sheridan said.

Moreno looked at Sheridan, his expression mocking. "You'll get blood on your pretty clothes."

"That doesn't bother me," Sheridan answered. "It's the blood of heroes."

Moreno rolled his eyes, said something in Spanish that made his goons laugh.

Gabe and Joaquin bent over the body of one of the security guards, lifted him, a white table cloth still covering him, offering him some dignity in death.

"We'll go down the staff elevator," Gabe told Joaquin. "It's around the corner and down the hall to my right."

"Got it."

For a time, they said nothing else, Moreno and his men watching them.

When they were out of the ballroom, Joaquin broke the silence, his voice a whisper. "I overheard that *chingadero* commander tell his men to shoot you if you refuse to leave. I think he sees you as trouble."

So Moreno was smarter than he looked.

"I can't leave Kat." But Gabe couldn't make her a widow either.

"She wants you to go. She says the kids need at least one parent."

He thought of Alissa and Nakai, suppressed rage flaring in his gut. He couldn't come home without their mother. "I'm not leaving her here."

He'd wanted to ask Moreno to let her go but had been afraid the bastard would make her pay for his actions the way he'd punished Kara for Sheridan's words.

Joaquin went on. "She doesn't want me to tell you this, but her water broke."

Gabe's pulse spiked. He stopped in his tracks. "*What?*"

She was a month early. If she'd gone into labor now, it might be a sign the baby was in some kind of distress. Last time she'd been checked, the baby had been breech and high in her pelvis. If it was still breech...

He had to get her out of here and to a hospital.

"*Cállate!*" One of Moreno's armed goons walked up beside them, spoke to Ramirez in Spanish.

Ramirez answered, the contempt in his voice clear even if Gabe couldn't understand his words.

The man glared at him, sticking with them as they stepped into the elevator and set the body on the floor, Sheridan and Carmichael behind them with a second. He rode down with them, then stood in the open elevator door as they carried the bodies outside, where a few ambulances remained, EMTs standing ready with body bags and gurneys.

He and Joaquin lifted the body onto the gurney. Then Gabe pretended to help one of the EMTs fit the body he'd helped carry into the bag, glancing surreptitiously around to make certain he wouldn't be overheard.

"Remember every word I'm about to say. Lives depend on it. Holly Andris was grazed on the head by an AK round. She's conscious and seems okay, but she probably has a concussion. Also, Kat James is eight months pregnant. Her water just broke. She's in premature labor and needs help. Tell whoever's in charge. Holly Andris. Kat James. And tell them not to mention me. I'm Gabe Rossiter. Can you remember that?"

The young man nodded. "Yes. Holly Andris. Kat James. Gabe Rossiter."

"Good man." Gabe walked back up the stairs to the loading dock, joining Ramirez, Sheridan, and Carmichael in the elevator, where they were once again under the hateful glare of Moreno's goon.

Gabe met Sheridan's gaze, saw the dark fury smoldering inside him. He knew that Sheridan was doing exactly what he was doing—weighing their chances against the bastard with the rifle. Four against one was good odds. But even if they managed to kill the son of a bitch, take his weapon, and mount some kind of resistance, Moreno wouldn't hesitate to take his rage out on the others, Kara most especially.

A muscle moved in Sheridan's jaw, and he broke eye contact.

Gabe had to do something. He couldn't leave his wife in the hands of killers. Having a baby was hard under the best circumstances. He'd been with Kat both times she'd given birth. The thought of her going through premature labor as a hostage...

He couldn't risk her or their baby.

Heart tripping, he started piecing together a plan. It wasn't a very good plan, but it was better than getting shot and much better than letting his wife suffer through childbirth as a prisoner of terrorists.

When they carried the last body out to the ambulance, he glanced around, looking for some way to conceal himself, some way to sneak back into the hotel from outside the loading dock. He spotted some thick steel I-beams just inside the door.

"Don't do anything loco," Ramirez whispered as they settled the last body onto a gurney.

"What makes you think I'm going to do something crazy?"

"Experience," Ramirez answered. "Also, you looked up. That means you're thinking about going vertical."

Ramirez knew him too well.

Gabe had spent his life before Kat sending every crag, slab, and big wall he could get his chalked fingers onto, building a reputation for himself as an extreme athlete and world-class free solo climber. Adrenaline had been his drug of choice. He'd used it to dull the hurt of his past, risking everything to stay ahead of the pain. And then Kat had come into his life, and his world had changed. He couldn't fail her.

"I need some kind of distraction."

Ramirez nodded. "You act like you're leaving, and I'll do what I can."

"Don't get shot."

"Right."

"If this doesn't work and I get my head blown off ..."

Ramirez nodded. "Take care, man."

"You, too." Gabe took a few backward steps as if he were about to climb into the back of the waiting ambulance.

Ramirez crossed to the stairs on the other side of the loading dock, ran up a few, then seemed to trip and fall. He gave a cry, rocking back and forth and holding his leg. All eyes turned his way.

Gabe saw his chance and took it, hurrying up the stairs and launching himself up one of the thick I-beams. He'd just reached the top and taken cover, when Moreno's thugs, apparently thinking Ramirez was trying to fake an injury so he could leave with one of the ambulances, dragged him to his feet and back through the door.

They seemed to have forgotten about Gabe entirely.

Thanks, Ramirez. I owe you big time.

Gabe watched Moreno's men as they lowered the big loading dock door, secured it, then posted two men to watch it from the inside, the rest disappearing into the elevator with Ramirez.

Okay, Rossiter. Now what?

20:10

MEGAN SAT IN THE living room, nursing Jackson, unable to take her gaze off the television, where Channel 12 was showing recycled footage of the Palace Hotel. Marc was in there somewhere, and no one knew if he was still alive.

How like her brother to put everyone else's safety ahead of his own. Hadn't he done the same with her? He'd saved her life then helped her get back on her feet after she'd almost destroyed herself.

She wouldn't be able to bear it if anything happened to him.

Poor Sophie. She must be terrified. She was the sweetest sister-in-law a person could hope to have. She'd put her life on the line for Megan and

Marc, going above and beyond her job as a journalist to find the truth that had set both of them free.

God, keep them safe. And please don't let Marc do anything too stupid.

But Megan knew her brother. When it came to protecting those he loved, he wouldn't hold back.

If anything happened to either of them...

No, she couldn't let her imagination go there. She couldn't.

Janet made her way down the stairs, holding the railing with one hand, her cane in the other. She sat beside Megan. "Anything new?"

Megan shook her head, cell phone on the coffee table in front of her. She'd asked Tessa to call her directly if she heard anything from Julian, who was now on the scene. "They're doing what news stations do when they don't have any news. They keep repeating the same thing. 'Terrorists have taken over the Palace Hotel. The Secretary of State and more than 300 others held hostage. Stay tuned for bloodshed.'"

Janet took her hand, gave it a squeeze. "They'll send in HRT. Those guys are the best-trained law-enforcement unit in the nation. They train with Delta Force and Navy SEALs. They'll do everything they can to free the hostages safely."

Megan took some comfort from Janet's words. Janet had been an FBI special agent until she'd taken a bullet to the hip. She probably knew more about what was going on at the Palace than Channel 12 news.

"I have an idea." Janet took the remote, switched to Laura Nilsson's station. Laura was married to Javier Corbray, Nate's best friend from his military days. She'd worked on the I-Team with the others for a while before taking a position as the main news anchor for a national station in

Washington, D.C. Watching her broadcasts always felt like getting the news from a friend.

"Thanks," Megan said.

From the mudroom, came the sound of Jack and Nate's voices as they took off their boots and coats after settling the horses for the night.

"Mommy, what is a 'hostage'?" asked Emily, who sat on the floor near the Christmas tree playing with her toy ponies.

Megan took a deep breath, wondering how she could explain this in a way that wouldn't trigger bad memories for her daughter. "A hostage is someone who is being kept prisoner by bad guys."

"Like that bad man who hurt you and made us stay in the basement?"

Megan swallowed, did her best to keep emotion out of her voice. "Yes. Like that."

Megan and Janet shared a glance, and Emily went on playing as if they hadn't just spoken of something terrible. She'd seen things that night no child should see—drugs, pornography, violence, death.

Then Emily spoke again. "Daddy saved us from the bad man. Maybe he should go save Uncle Marc and Aunt Sophie, too."

"Maybe." Megan couldn't help but smile. Emily loved Nate so very much. One day Megan would have to tell her daughter that the man Nate had saved them from that night had been her biological father.

Nate walked in through the kitchen, thick woolen socks on his feet, his cheeks red from the cold. His gaze met Megan's. "Any word?"

Megan shook her head.

Nate reached down, ran a finger over Jackson's chubby cheek, his gaze shifting to Emily. "They have police there to help save your Uncle Marc and Aunt Sophie."

So he'd heard what she'd said.

"Is Uncle Julie there?"

Nate and Janet hid smiles.

"Yes. Uncle Zach is there, too."

Jack stepped out of the kitchen. "Anyone care for coffee?"

"Yeah," Nate said. "Thanks."

Megan's cell phone rang, making her heart skip.

Nate picked it up, held it out for her.

Pulse tripping, she answered. "This is Megan."

"It's Tessa. Marc is alive. Julian said Marc got in touch with Chief Irving again and that he'd been grazed by a bullet but was okay. He took down four guys on the roof and kept them from setting up a machine gun to use against the police. He's a hero, Megan."

"*Thank God!*" Megan blinked back tears of relief.

But Marc had always been a hero in her eyes.

CHAPTER SEVEN

20:15

Holly sat with her back against the wall, holding a makeshift ice bag to her head, Matt's dinner jacket around her shoulders—a sweet, protective gesture on his part. Sophie had given her a couple of aspirins, and that had helped a little with the headache. It had done nothing for her nausea.

By now, Gabe was free. He would've told Nick that she'd been hurt but was okay. That would keep Nick from doing something stupid. Then again, a part of her really wanted him to do something stupid and brave and heroic to get her and all her friends out of here alive, especially Kat.

Joaquin and Sophie had made a place for her back in the corner, Alex, Joaquin, and even Tom donating their dinner jackets so she could lie on something other than the carpet. She said her contractions were mild, but Holly could see she was afraid.

"Last time I was checked, the baby was breech," she whispered to Sophie. "What if it's still breech? What if the cord is prolapsed? I don't want to lose this baby."

Sophie sat beside Kat, holding her hand. "Can you still feel it moving?"

Kat pressed a hand against her belly, rubbed it. "Yes."

"Try to relax and focus on that."

Holly didn't understand all of that. She didn't know much about pregnancy or birth, despite the fact she'd been with Kara when her daughter Caitlyn was born—an experience that had left Holly more afraid to become a mother than excited. But right now, she was afraid for Kat.

They needed to get her out of here or at least move her someplace quiet and private where she could lie down on a *real* bed. To make that happen, they needed to tell Commander Asshat that she was in labor. But Kat was afraid he'd use that against her or find a way to hurt her or her baby.

Holly couldn't blame her for worrying. Once Moreno knew about her situation, there was no telling what he would do. He might let her go. He might shoot her. From what Holly had heard, the bastard enjoyed watching people suffer and didn't care whom he hurt—innocent men, women, even children.

At the same time, they couldn't wait for a rescue to get Kat out of here. Holly knew it would be many hours, perhaps even days or weeks before this ended. There was no way the US government would negotiate with narco-terrorists. They wouldn't release Moreno's cousin, and they wouldn't give him $35 million. It would be a long, drawn-out stalemate—unless Moreno held true to his threats and started shooting. If that happened, HRT would move in hard and fast.

She watched Moreno, saw Joaquin standing as near to the bastard as he could get. He was the only one among them who spoke fluent Spanish. He'd been trying to eavesdrop to gather intel. So far he'd learned that Moreno was angry with the crew on the roof, but Joaquin wasn't sure why.

Moreno had also sent a couple of men down to watch over the "little Christmas present below."

Holly had no idea what Moreno meant by that, but she was pretty sure it wasn't the kind of gift one would hope to get from Santa.

She watched Moreno, trying to glean insights that might help her, certain she'd seen him somewhere before. He strode from one end of the room to the other, talking with his men, AK propped against his shoulder, red beret perched stupidly on his head. But what kind of man was he?

He'd grown up in a patriarchal family where the authority of the male head of the household went unchallenged. How small he must have felt, living under his uncle's fist, subject to the extremes of his uncle's personality. He'd grown up amid violence, had probably witnessed brutality as a kid, becoming desensitized to it. He'd been emotionally castrated by the power his uncle held over him, never able to be his own man, always having to follow orders. It had turned him into a rage-filled narcissist. But here, with hundreds of people's lives in his hands, he felt important. He was finally the male authority figure, finally free to give the orders—and vent a lifetime of anger.

He didn't hesitate to hurt women. She'd seen that when he'd struck poor Kara. He'd probably grown up viewing women as objects for male use—wives born to serve husbands, whores paid to endure whatever got their clients off, mothers who doted on their sons, daughters to be coddled and controlled like living dolls. He liked his women meek, submissive.

The way to his heart wasn't through sex or money, but his ego. That's how it was with all narcissists. His reaction to everyone and everything depended on how it made him feel about himself.

As if he could sense her perusal, he turned his head and looked straight into her eyes. And then he walked her way.

"Don't take any unnecessary risks, Bradshaw," Tom said, calling her by her maiden name. "You've done enough."

"I didn't know you cared." She let Matt's jacket slip from her shoulders, willed tears into her eyes, whispered to her friends. "No matter what happens, do *not* interfere."

People moved aside for him and the henchman who followed after him until he was standing before her.

She looked up.

"Get up," he said.

She set the ice bag down, started to get to her feet, deliberately falling onto her knees before him, her face directly in front of his crotch. She looked up at him through wide, tear-filled eyes, then struggled to her feet, wobbling a bit on her heels.

He reached out a hand and steadied her.

Gotcha, you son of a bitch.

"One of my men says he saw you pull the fire alarm. How did you find out about our little party?"

She avoided looking into his eyes, did her best to act terrified. "I-I bumped into one of those carts—you know, the ones the waiters push. I guess I'd had too much to drink. A g-gun slid out the side of it. I tried telling the guards, b-but they didn't believe me. I didn't know what else to do, so ... P-please don't hurt me."

He studied her, held up her ID. "You're not a journalist?"

"N-no, sir. I'm not a reporter. I came as someone's date. I'm ... I'm ..." She hesitated, then lowered her voice to a whisper. "I'm an escort."

Moreno frowned, his lips slowly curving into a twisted smirk. "You're a whore."

Holly let color come into her cheeks. "An escort. I don't get paid to do *that.*"

"Who is your date?" He glanced around, then pointed straight at Matt. "Oh, yes. I remember. You."

And Holly realized why she recognized him. He'd been posing as a valet when they'd arrived. He'd seen her walk in with Matt.

Matt wisely said nothing, his jaw tensing.

Moreno sneered at him. "I can see why you have to pay for pussy."

Holly met Matt's gaze, felt a pang of regret for him.

I'm sorry, Matt!

Then Moreno turned and spoke in Spanish to his men, sliding his arm around her shoulder and leading her away from the others.

She wasn't yet sure what her plan was, but so far it seemed to be going well.

20:17

JULIAN WANTED TO HIT something. Hunter had just risked his life and saved God only knew how many cops and SWAT guys, and the FBI's SWAT commander wanted him to stand down. He stood toe to toe with Dixon, looked into the man's eyes. "Maybe he should just surrender to the terrorists, take responsibility for the men he killed, and let them blow his head off."

"Darcangelo!" Chief Irving shouted. "No one is saying that Hunter should turn himself over to Moreno."

"Right now he's the only one doing a goddamned thing to stop these guys."

Dixon's voice was entirely devoid of emotion. "HRT is on its way."

The door opened, a blast of frigid air rushing through the cramped space.

Andris entered, followed by Tower and a man wearing an EMS uniform.

One of Dixon's men stopped them. "Dixon says you two aren't allowed in the vehicle."

"I've got intel from the inside." Andris pushed past him. "This man just came from the Palace, where he spoke with Gabe Rossiter."

Dixon frowned. "Who the hell is Gabe Rossiter?"

"A former park ranger," Julian answered. "I worked with him a few years back. He's got solid law-enforcement skills."

"Let's hear it, son," Irving said to the EMT.

"He told me to remember what he was about to say as if lives depended on it. He said Holly Andris was grazed on the head by the bullet from an AK. He said she's conscious and seems okay but might have a concussion."

Julian met Andris's gaze, saw a muscle clench in his jaw.

An AK round?

Jesus.

That had been damned close.

"He said Kat James is eight months pregnant and that her water had just broken. He said she's in premature labor and needs help."

Son of a bitch.

Julian had forgotten that Kat was heavily pregnant. He couldn't imagine a woman going through labor in that environment. Why hadn't the fuckers released her together with the wounded?

"There's more," Tower said.

"He wanted me to tell all of this to whoever's in charge, but also to tell you not to mention him to the terrorists."

Dixon frowned. "Why would he say that?"

"Kat James is his wife," Andris explained. "One of the wounded men said the terrorists are hurting the women to control the men. When Lt. Gov. Sheridan spoke up, Moreno backhanded his wife, nearly knocking her off her feet."

And *that* made Julian want to kill the son of a bitch with his bare hands.

He couldn't imagine what Rossiter was going through. "He probably wants to make sure Kat isn't made to pay for his having shared this intel with us."

"Here's the weird thing," the EMT said. "The terrorists tried to send Rossiter away with us, but he didn't want to go. He had his friend create a distraction, and he disappeared back inside the hotel. He jumped up on a support beam and just disappeared. He was gone, like Spider-Man or something."

Julian met McBride's gaze, saw the corners of his mouth turn up in a grin at the EMT's description.

Dixon's eyes narrowed. "He *disappeared*?"

McBride nodded. "Rossiter is a world-class climber. He has free-soloed routes that most elite climbers wouldn't dream of trying without ropes."

Dixon's eyebrows rose. "Why in God's name would he go back inside?"

Julian crossed his arms over his chest. "Are you married, Dixon?"

Dixon shook his head.

That's what Julian had thought. The man had no idea what it was like to love a woman more than he loved himself, to be bound to her body and soul, to see her in his children's faces, to know down to his bones that she was the axis of his world.

"He went back inside to try to find a way to protect and free his *pregnant wife*." Julian had to fight not to shout. "You've got two men on the inside now, two good men. There's a woman in premature labor and more than three hundred other people in mortal danger. Are you going to leave Hunter freezing his ass off on the roof and risk losing the intel those cell phones might bring us?"

"Let us go up in the Little Bird." Andris was pleading with him now. "You can have police sirens make a din if you want. They won't hear us. We can collect the weapons and the phones, give Hunter some body armor—"

"No!" Dixon's voice boomed through the confined space. "We wait for HRT."

Andris's expression hardened. He turned without a word and stalked out of the trailer with Tower, slamming the door behind them.

Fed up with this bullshit and afraid of what might come out of his mouth next, Julian followed them, cold air hitting him in the face. Andris and Tower were talking, their heads bent together.

McBride came up behind Julian. "Want to take bets about what those two are planning?"

"Whatever it is, I want in." He looked northward, saw the top of the Palace Hotel through the bare branches of the trees.

Hang on, Hunter. You're not alone.

20:20

MARC KNEW HE WAS no longer alone. Someone had come up the stairs and stepped out of the bulkhead. He'd heard the door squeak on its hinges.

Chilled to the bone, he stepped back out of the light, dropped to one knee, raised the TAC-338.

A man in camo emerged from behind the bulkhead, some kind of rifle held in one hand, its muzzle pointing down. "Luis!"

He'd probably been sent topside to find out what the hell was going on. But Marc couldn't let them figure it out. Not yet.

He sighted on the man and pulled the trigger, dropping him with a shot to center mass.

Five.

That left at least 19 assorted assholes still at large in the hotel.

Marc kicked the body, made sure the fucker was dead, then confiscated the man's wallet, cell phone, and the wool gloves he found in his jacket pocket. He dragged the body into the shadows with the others, then walked back over to the M2, which he'd been ordered to strip.

He knelt down, jerked off the weapon's backplate.

So the FBI wanted him to stand down, did they? They wanted him to hide somewhere while a bunch of murdering motherfuckers held hundreds of people, including his wife and some of his best friends, at gunpoint?

Right. Sure. Fine.

He stood and hurled the backplate over the side of the building, a desperate roar tearing itself from his throat. He watched as it arced through the darkness, falling eight stories and landing with a metallic clank in the deserted street below.

Goddamn it!

Sophie!

If only he'd kept her with him. If only he hadn't sent her away.

He couldn't change the decisions he'd made. All he could do now was be a good cop and follow orders.

Or not.

He turned back to the M2 and set about disassembling it down to its most basic components, fighting to rein in his anger. He understood the FBI's strategy. They didn't want the FLC to misunderstand his actions and start slaughtering people. But if he hid inside, he'd be surrendering the high ground to the enemy. They didn't have to have the M2 to kill cops. Anyone with decent aim and a rifle could kill from up here.

He got to his feet, his toes now numb from the cold, and got to work scattering pieces of the M2, dropping screws down vents, sliding bigger pieces down rain gutters, and tossing pieces off different sides of the building.

He wasn't sure what to do with the confiscated cell phones, which buzzed like angry hornets in his pocket. If only he spoke Spanish, he'd know what these bastards were saying to each other. He would be able to buy more time by texting back and making whoever was in charge of this clusterfuck think that his team on the roof was still in action. Too bad he couldn't tap into Darcangelo's brain. He spoke Spanish like it was his mother tongue and...

Mind racing, Marc hurled the heavy barrel of the M2 over the side of the building, then pulled his cell phone out of his pocket. He settled himself with the TAC-338 where he had a clear view of the bulkhead so that he'd see anyone who came up to the roof. Then he dialed Darcangelo's cell and found himself fighting to talk through chattering teeth. "H-hey, I've got an idea."

"Hunter? Shut up and listen to me."

"Y-you haven't even h-heard my idea yet."

But Darcangelo just kept talking, his voice quiet as if he didn't want to be overheard. "Andris and Derek Tower are on their way. They've got an MH-6 Little Bird on standby at the Centennial Airport and should reach you within the hour. You won't hear them until they're right on top of you. Their bird has serious stealth features."

This was the best fucking news Marc could have hoped for.

"D-dixon changed his m-mind." It was getting seriously hard to talk.

"No. This is an unauthorized operation. *I* don't even know about it."

Wait. What?

Marc thought his brain must have frozen. "It's n-not authorized?"

"Nope. Dixon and Irving have no idea."

"Wow." Marc was touched. It took serious balls to defy the FBI. Then he remembered. "Andris. H-he's coming for H-holly."

"Holly is awake. We got intel saying she was grazed by an AK round and might have a concussion. Oh, and try not to shoot Rossiter. He got away and is on the loose in there somewhere. Kat went into premature labor. We need to get her out."

"Wow," Marc said again.

Shit.

The cold was really getting to him.

"Is there somewhere up there where you can warm up? You sound like you're hypothermic."

Darcangelo was right.

Marc glanced around. "Th-there's a g-greenhouse."

"Get your ass inside."

"D-don't you want to hear m-my idea?" He got to his aching feet and moved carefully toward the greenhouse, keeping his gaze fixed on the bulkhead, aware that he was distracted and that his mind and reflexes were compromised by exposure.

"Sure. Go ahead." Darcangelo sounded like he was talking to a child now.

"I-I need you t-to be m-my Spanish t-translator."

"Your ... what?"

"I h-have the c-cell phones. If I r-respond, I can d-delay them from c-coming up h-here and f-finding out what h-happened."

For a moment, Darcangelo said nothing. "You know, for a human ice block, you're not too stupid."

"F-fuck you, D-dickangelo."

"Sorry, buddy. The answer is still no."

CHAPTER EIGHT

20:25

Reece sat in a chair beside Kara, wrapped more ice in his handkerchief. "Here."

"Thanks." She pressed it against her swollen cheek, her eye already black.

"How's your head?"

"It still hurts." She gave him a little smile that didn't quite reach her eyes, and he knew she was more shaken than she was letting on. "I'll be okay."

"What is he going to do with that girl?" a man whispered.

Across the ballroom, that son of a bitch Moreno had his arm around Holly's shoulders. He looked her up and down, talking to her in the tone of voice one might use for a small child.

Go ahead, asshole. Underestimate her. I dare you.

"I don't know."

Reece couldn't say it aloud, but that *girl* had more skill for dealing with situations like this one than anyone else in the room. He'd watched her go into action, transforming in the blink of an eye into a helpless, passive blonde to get close to Moreno. Well, she was close all right.

What was her plan?

Reece wished he knew. He was pretty certain Andris wouldn't want Holly taking risks like this. Then again, if not for her, the bastards would have taken Ambassador DeLacy and hundreds of others hostage.

Be careful, Holly.

Moreno and his men had no respect for women. Proof of that marred Kara's face.

Hatred churned hot and bitter in Reece's gut. He should have seen the blow coming. He should have blocked it. He should have made certain Kara was nowhere near him before he'd opened his mouth.

Damn it.

He had no doubt that Moreno's threat to hand her over to his men was real. He couldn't imagine there was much the son of a bitch wouldn't do. Still, the fucker would have to go through him if he wanted to touch Kara again.

Big words, Sheridan.

The truth was that Moreno could order a couple of his men to restrain Reece and then do whatever he wanted to do to Kara.

Reece had never felt so completely helpless, so utterly powerless.

Moreno knew it, and he was gloating.

He watched as the bastard led Holly over to the table where Secretary Holmes sat and offered her a chair. For a moment, Reece was afraid Secretary Holmes would give Holly away. He knew the two of them were acquainted. But Holmes was smarter than that and fast on the uptake. She acted as if she'd never met Holly before.

"Do you think Secretary Holmes will do it?" Kara whispered. "Will she order his cousin's release?"

Reece shook his head. "She can't—not legally."

She'd tried to explain that to Moreno once already, but he didn't give a damn about the intricacies of the US judicial system. In his world, the men with power and money made the rules and did as they chose. From his point of view, Secretary Holmes had spearheaded the capture and extradition of his cousin, and that meant she had the power to release him again.

What would he do to Secretary Holmes—what would he do to all of them—when he realized he was wrong?

Hopefully, HTR would arrive before they found out. Then it would be Moreno and his men who were afraid for their lives.

20:25

GABE LOOKED DOWN AT the two assholes who'd been left to guard the loading dock. He'd worked his way along the ceiling using the I-beams and other supports and now stood directly above them. They spoke to one another in Spanish, never looking up, never stepping more than a couple of feet away from one another.

You're not going to make this easy for me are you?

Gabe had run a few scenarios through his mind, most of which ended with him getting shot and dying on the concrete floor. He couldn't let that happen. Kat thought he was safe and maybe home now, caring for Alissa and Nakai. He didn't want her to get the bad news later that he'd gotten himself killed doing something stupid, leaving her to raise their kids alone.

It's only stupid if you fuck up and get shot.

Right.

He had the element of surprise and a titanium leg that could do a fair amount of damage, but they had assault rifles and probably a hidden knife or two. He was pretty sure he'd be able to take them out one at a time, but two at once?

Come on, guys. Someone take a bathroom break.

It had been years since he'd done DT training—defensive tactics. Once it had been a regular part of his annual training cycle. But when he'd lost his leg, he'd left his job as a park ranger, taking a job test-driving prosthetic limbs built for athletes so that he'd have more time for Kat. He was still in good shape, but he was a little rusty when it came to fighting.

It will come back to you. It's just like riding a bike.

Beating the shit out of people. Riding a bike. No difference there.

Then one of the assholes turned his back on the other and began to stroll toward the other side of the loading dock door.

Yes!

For a moment, Gabe worried the guy would stop or turn back, but he kept going, looking back over his shoulder as if to see whether the other one was watching him. Then he pulled something from his pocket that he didn't seem to want his buddy to see—a small container of white powder.

Cocaine.

Gabe saw his chance.

He waited for the cokehead to snort, then dropped silently onto the man below.

His feet came down on the man's shoulders, driving him face-first into the concrete, knocking the rifle from his hands. Gabe fell forward, rolled, then leaped to his feet and grabbed for the weapon. His hands closed around it, the steel cold. He raised it, worked the bolt, then turned it toward the cokehead, who was fumbling with his rifle, his panic and the rush of the drug making him clumsy.

Gabe fired a double tap, the blast deafening in the enclosed space. Then he turned the weapon on the man he'd jumped, only to discover that the son of a bitch was out cold. He pressed the barrel of the rifle to the man's head, finger on the trigger.

Why was he hesitating?

Do it! Do. It.

He lowered the rifle.

It was one thing to kill a man who was about to open fire on him. It was something else entirely to kill someone who was unconscious.

Gabe hooked the AK strap over his shoulder, bent down, and searched the man, taking his cell phone, wallet, and a sweet little switchblade. Then he stripped him down to his underwear and dragged him toward the side door. He shoved the bastard out into the cold of the dark alley. "You can thank me later."

He left the door ajar and pressed the button to raise the loading dock door. Then he took the bastard's cell phone and dialed 911. "I'm calling from inside the Palace Hotel. Put me through to Police Chief Irving."

20:30

"THERE'S AN OLD WOMAN who says she is diabetic and needs insulin. Also, there is a pregnant woman lying down in the back corner who seems to be having trouble. There are many who say they need to use the toilet and—"

"*¡Cállate!*" Pepe cut Andrés off, anger making his face burn. No commander should have to deal with this kind of petty bullshit. He lowered his voice, speaking in Spanish. "You and Santiago see to it that people are taken to the toilets, but keep a close eye on them all. If anyone escapes, it will be on your head."

"What about the diabetic and the pregnant—"

"I don't give a damn about them." He dismissed Andrés and turned his attention back to the bitch who was to blame for all of this.

"I can make the call, but it's not going to do you any good." Holmes sounded calm, but there were beads of sweat on her forehead. "This is a nation of laws, sir. Your cousin broke the plea agreement himself. He was convicted by a jury and sentenced to prison in a court of law. I simply don't have the authority to set him free."

Pepe leaned in, looked into her lying eyes. "You are the reason he rots in prison! You will free him, or you will watch everyone here die before I kill you myself!"

Rage flowed through him like rum, the rush sweet and warm.

"Oh, just make the call!" said the pretty little slut. "You're going to make him angry, and he'll start hurting people."

Pepe turned to stare at her, amused that she would speak so boldly to a government official. She was too stupid even to know her place. He found himself chuckling. "What is your name again?"

She looked up at him through those big eyes, not so bold now that she had his attention. "Holly."

He let his gaze travel over her, wishing he could get five minutes alone with her. *Ay, carajo,* she was beautiful! That mouth. Those tits. He'd fuck her so hard she wouldn't be able to walk afterward, and he would enjoy it.

And if she didn't want him?

He would enjoy it even more.

Pepe met Holmes' gaze. "This little slut is smarter than you are. You would be wise to listen to her."

"I'm not a slut. I told you."

Secretary Holmes' eyes flashed, and she glared at the whore. "Do you really think that will do us any good?"

Pepe found her response strange. It wasn't her words so much as the way she said them—as if she expected the whore to have an answer that mattered.

His cell phone buzzed.

A message from Camilo.

I caught them smoking marimba. Told them I'd shoot them myself if they didn't get the job done. All is well up here now.

Relief that the machine gun was in place warred with his rage at Luis for defying his command not to use drugs during the operation.

He texted back.

Tell Luis I will make him eat his own balls if they disappoint me again. Get your ass back down here. Send Yeison and his team to take over for Luis. Have Luis and the others go below to clear their heads.

He pocketed his mobile phone, a vision of those lips wrapped around his cock sending a rush of blood to his groin.

Tavo ran up to him. "*Jefe*, that fat man over there says he thinks he's having a heart attack. He says—"

"*¡Malparidos!*" Pepe momentarily forgot about the slut, grabbed his AK, and fired it at the ceiling, anger filling him with vigor. "The next person to complain to one of my men that his head hurts or he has a stomach ache or he is not feeling so well is going to get shot. Do you understand?"

"Come." He grabbed the slut's wrist, drew her to her feet, pulled her after him toward the door.

"Wh-where are we going?"

She couldn't be *that* stupid.

"This is a hotel, no? We're getting a room."

"I'll make the call!"

Pepe stopped, turned to find Sheridan walking toward him.

"I'll make the call," Sheridan repeated. "Secretary Holmes might not be able to secure your cousin's release, but I can."

20:35

SOPHIE STOOD ROOTED TO the spot, almost unable to breathe. She'd asked one of their captors to ask Moreno to release Kat, only to watch Moreno go berserk, shooting bullets into the ceiling, dragging Holly toward the door. Both Joaquin and Reece had jumped to their feet, Tom, Alex, and Matt, too, and Sophie had been certain someone was about to get shot. Then Reece had shouted out for Moreno.

Now he stood face to face with the bastard, who still held Holly by the wrist.

"How can you do something she cannot?"

"I'm the number two ranking official in the state." Reece seemed so cool, not afraid at all. "That places me high in the chain of command over all state prisons. The men who run Supermax don't report to the Secretary of State. They report to the governor—and to me."

That was an outright lie. ADX was a federal facility. Reece had no authority over the facility or its staff.

Would Moreno understand that?

Then Sophie saw her.

Kara stood back in the crowd, her face bruised, fear in her eyes. She wasn't afraid for herself, Sophie knew, but for Reece. He'd only done this to stop Moreno from hurting Holly. But if Moreno realized Reece was lying ...

God forbid.

Moreno released Holly, then gestured for Reece to sit at the table beside Secretary Holmes and handed him a cell phone. "If you can make this happen, then do it."

Reece took the phone, dialed a number. "Armstrong, hey, it's Lt. Gov. Sheridan. Are you following what's happening at the Palace Hotel tonight?"

Armstrong was the director of the Department of Corrections. He had no authority or involvement over ADX either.

"Put it on speaker," Moreno demanded.

Reece did as he was asked.

"Yes, I am, sir. Are you—"

"I am authorizing you to release Oscar Moreno Ortíz into the custody of the US Marshals Service for immediate transport from Supermax to the Palace Hotel via helicopter. Be certain he arrives well before midnight. Do you understand?"

Armstrong stammered for a moment. "Yes, sir."

"I'm counting on you to make it happen." Reece ended the call, handed the phone back to Moreno.

"I guess I'm glad I let you live," the bastard said.

A quiet whimper caught Sophie's attention.

Kat.

She walked back to the corner, found Kat breathing through another contraction, her face tight with pain. Sophie sat beside her, took her hand, wishing she could do more. She'd had two homebirths and knew how terribly painful unmedicated birth could be. But her births had been full-term, normal births, and she'd been safe in her own home with Marc beside her, not trapped in a hotel with terrorists.

When the contraction had passed, Kat opened her eyes. "I'm glad you didn't push him. I don't want you or anyone else to get shot."

Sophie didn't want that either. "I'm sorry."

"They're getting stronger. They're right on top of each other." Kat's voice was calm, but there was fear in her eyes. "I haven't felt the baby move for a while."

"Drink." Sophie handed her a bottle of water, tried to sound reassuring, remembering the things Marc had said to comfort her when she'd been in labor. "Just take them one at a time. Try to rest."

Inside, she felt like screaming, rage and worry knotting in her stomach.

Damn it!

This wasn't fair. It wasn't right. No woman should have to go through this. And if the baby really was breech or wasn't ready for the world…

How far along did Kat say she was?

Thirty-five weeks.

That was early, but not terrifyingly scary early.

Where was the cavalry? Where was SWAT?

And, dear God, where is Marc?

She didn't think he was dead. He hadn't been found among the bodies Gabe and the others had carried out, or someone would have told her. She hoped he'd gotten out and was preparing to storm this place with his team, working out a plan to rescue them. Or maybe he was watching over them from the shadows.

Be careful, babe.

20:42

MARC SAT NEXT TO the electric heater, soaking in the warmth and typing in the letters Darcangelo told him to type, his toes still pinched from the cold. At least his teeth were no longer chattering. "How do you spell 'cocksucker'?"

"Dixon authorized us to make it seem like these guys were still alive. He didn't say we could provoke them."

"You sure know how to ruin a guy's fun."

But none of this was fun, Marc's thoughts never leaving Sophie for a moment, never straying from the friends who were still in danger.

Now that he'd responded to Moreno's latest message to that dead fucker Camilo, he went back to sifting through Camilo's text messages, reading them over the phone to Darcangelo, who was writing them down and passing them on to the FBI.

"There's a group SMS. It says, '*El regalo de Navidad en el sótano está listo.*'" Marc recognized some of the words because Darcangelo had translated them before. "That's the fourth mention of a Christmas present in the basement. Someone needs to get down there and figure out what the hell they have waiting for us. My money says it's explosives."

"Yeah." Darcangelo sounded distracted. "We just got word that Sheridan ordered officials at Supermax to release Oscar Moreno Ortíz."

"He doesn't have the authority to do that."

"No, he doesn't, but Dixon thinks it's best if we act like he does. Sheridan isn't an idiot. If he did this, he did it for a reason."

For once, Marc agreed with Dixon.

Then Marc's phone vibrated, and he saw that Darcangelo had sent him a text message via WhatsApp.

They're almost there. Stay put. They're going to clear the roof. They know where you are.

It was about fucking time.

"Are you going to fry for this?" Marc didn't want that. Darcangelo was his best friend. He didn't want to see him get sacked.

"We should disconnect, save your battery. Keep your head down."

That wasn't an answer. Then again, with Dixon and his FBI suits sitting nearby, Darcangelo probably couldn't say much.

"Right. Will do." Marc ended the call.

Light flooded the greenhouse, the whir of a helo's rotors breaking up the silence as it came to a hover just north of the little greenhouse.

He pocketed the cell phones and got to his knees, hands behind his head, dark shapes dropping from the helo as four men fast-roped to the rooftop. He heard the tromp of boots, and the greenhouse door was thrown open, cold air flooding in.

A man in black wearing NVGs and carrying an M4A1 stepped inside. He lowered the weapon. "You can put your hands down now, Hunter."

Andris.

He dropped a bag of gear in front of Marc. "I thought you might want this."

"Glad you guys decided to show up."

"We'd have been here sooner if not for FBI bullshit."

Marc knew they had to work quickly. Even with the most advanced stealth technology, a helo sitting overhead was not quiet. The longer the bird was perched here, the greater the chance that someone inside would hear it.

He handed the cell phones over to Andris, who passed them on to someone else, then he stripped out of the dead guy's jacket, telling Andris what he'd done with the Browning M2 and the RPG-7.

"You ought to take care of that graze." Andris pointed. "It's pretty deep."

Marc touched his fingers to his side, saw that the wound was still oozing blood. "Got duct tape?"

"Always." Andris dug through his gear and tossed Marc a roll.

Marc had just pasted a strip of tape over his skin, sealing the wound, when someone came up behind Andris.

"It looks like there was one hell of a firefight up here." Derek Tower ducked inside the greenhouse, his rifle's stock in his shoulder, its muzzle pointed down. "Clever idea—putting your shirt on a dead man."

"Under the circumstances, I thought it looked better on him."

By the time Marc was dressed and strapped, the helo was gone, the cell phones, M2 ammo and other ordinance with it, the night silent once more. He checked his rifle and reloaded the magazine for his SIG. "What's the plan?"

CHAPTER NINE

20:45

*Z*ach took a swig of coffee, listening while Irving briefed them on the latest.

"Two of my SWAT guys found the bastard exactly where Rossiter said we would. He was semi-conscious, so we haven't gotten anything from him beyond his name. He's on his way to University Hospital with a suspected skull fracture, a dislocated shoulder, and hypothermia."

"What about Rossiter?" Dixon asked.

"No sign of him. He left the door to the loading dock wide open. We found a DB inside. No weapons. I assume Rossiter took them."

"He threw the back door open and cleared the way," Darcangelo said. "That sounds like an invitation."

"Yeah, but it's one we can't accept—not yet." Dixon clearly wasn't happy. "Do you have any way to get in touch with Rossiter? He needs to stand down and leave the hotel before he gets himself or someone else killed."

"I've tried calling the number he used when he called me, but he's not answering," Irving said.

Zach knew that it wouldn't matter anyway. Rossiter wouldn't leave the hotel as long as Kat was a hostage.

Dixon didn't like it. "Now we've got six dead terrorists, one in the hospital, and a serious problem when Moreno finds out. How are we going to convince him that the FBI and SWAT aren't behind all of this?"

As much as Zach hated to admit it, Dixon had a point. They needed to have some kind of response for the moment when Moreno discovered he was short seven men. And yet, he couldn't blame Hunter or Rossiter for doing what they'd done.

If Moreno had Natalie…

Zach couldn't go there.

Darcangelo spoke up. "We could tell him that one of the hotel guests, who just happens to be an ex-cop or something, got away and that it has nothing to do with us. What we *can't* do is identify either Hunter or Rossiter."

That much was clear. Sophie and Kat would pay if Moreno could connect them to his dead and missing men.

Dixon frowned. "Moreno is smart. What's to stop him from checking what we tell him against the hotel's records? To pull that off, we'd need a name, a room number, maybe even background—something more than just our word."

Dixon's intel guy stood. "We could hack into the hotel system, plant a name, build cover through social media, and create an identity from the ground up."

"Get started. I'll see what HRT says when they get here, but that sounds like a plan." Dixon turned to Zach. "Are you ready on your end?"

Zach nodded. "I'm leaving for the airport in a few minutes. I'll fly down to Florence, borrow Oscar Moreno Ortíz from Supermax, give him some pretty clothes, and fly him toward Denver. Once we're airborne, I'll have him talk to his cousin and confirm that he's free and on his way. Of course, we'll take the scenic route and won't make it to Denver. As soon as you give me the all-clear, we'll turn the bird back toward Florence and lock Ortíz back in his cell."

It was a risky plan, but Moreno hadn't left them with a lot of options. They needed to buy time for HRT to do its thing, and if taking Ortíz for a little flight accomplished that, Zach was happy to help out. There was no chance that Ortíz could escape, not with a half-dozen deputy marshals on board.

A man in an FBI SWAT uniform burst through the door. "Sir, there's a helo inbound and headed straight for the hotel."

Zach met Darcangelo's gaze, neither of them saying a word.

So, Andris and Tower had gone through with it.

No surprise there.

"What? I didn't hear—" Dixon was cut off by the thrum of a helicopter flying overhead. He glared at Irving. "You need to rein in your guys."

Irving pulled himself up to his full height. "Cobra doesn't report to me. If you want to rein them in, call the fucking Pentagon!"

"Goddamn private contractors! What's their plan? Are they at least going to pull Hunter off that roof?"

"How would I know?" Irving asked.

Zach glanced at his watch. "I need to head out."

He left Dixon and Irving to bicker, Darcangelo following him out the door.

"Good luck, McBride." Darcangelo held out his hand, and they shook.

In the distance, the Little Bird lifted off the top of the hotel and disappeared.

"You two, wait!" Irving called after them.

Uh-oh.

Irving strode over to them, clearly pissed as hell. "Did you know about this?"

Zach looked at Darcangelo, then back at Irving. "Define 'know.'"

"Jesus." Irving turned to Darcangelo, got right in his face. "Did you have knowledge beforehand that Cobra planned to defy the FBI and head up to the rooftop of the hotel with a goddamn helo?"

Darcangelo opened his mouth to answer.

"Oh, for Christ's sake!" Irving cut him off. "Never mind. I guess the less I know, the better."

In the distance came the thrum of a helo's rotors—not a Little Bird, but something much bigger. A Blackhawk came into view from the northeast.

"It's about damned time," Darcangelo muttered.

The Hostage Rescue Team had finally arrived.

21:05

HOLLY SAT IN THE nearest chair and rubbed her temple, her head throbbing.

Nearby, Moreno was talking on his cell phone with the FBI negotiator, who had called to tell him US Marshals were on their way to get his cousin.

Reece was working his way toward her, his movements casual, as if he were simply tired of standing around.

Holly wasn't sure whether she should thank him for the reprieve or smack him upside the head. Moreno had intended to rape her—that was obvious—but she'd been trained to deal with that possibility. A woman had a lot of power over a man whose penis and testicles were hanging out. With any luck, she might have been able to neutralize the bastard, cutting the head off this little viper and leaving his men leaderless.

Not that she hadn't been scared. Moreno was a sociopath. He would probably enjoy hurting her or even killing her. But she wasn't going to let her fear keep her from doing whatever she could to get her friends out of this alive.

Moreno had his back to her now, shouting into the phone. "No one is going anywhere until I get both my cousin and that thirty-five million!"

Reece came to stand behind her, spoke quietly. "He'll kill you, Holly."

A frisson of fear shot through her. "Let me worry about me, okay?"

"How's your head."

"It hurts." But that didn't matter right now. "Kat's in labor."

"*Jesus.*"

"What do you mean 'show of faith'?" Moreno shouted. "I let you take the wounded and dead. I have given you something. What have you given me?"

The man was volatile and more than a little drunk on power.

He turned and looked straight at Holly. "She is well, I assure you. She stays."

The FBI was trying to get her out, but Moreno wouldn't have it.

And Holly knew he wasn't done with her.

"What is her name?" He began craning his neck, as if looking for someone. He lowered the phone. "Bring me Kat James."

Holly found herself on her feet, headache forgotten.

One by one, the newspaper's staff turned to look at the back corner—everyone but Joaquin, whose jaw was set, his eyes hard, his gaze fixed on Moreno.

"What do you want with her?" he asked.

But Moreno saw her now.

So did Holly.

She lay on her side, breathing through a contraction, her eyes closed.

Sophie stood. "She can't walk or answer right now. She's having a contraction."

"Then I guess she cannot leave."

"I'll carry her." Joaquin walked back to the corner, lifted Kat into his arms.

One of Moreno's men spoke to his boss, Holly recognizing only a few words: *jefe, indios, Navaja.*

Joaquin crossed the room, stopping a few yards away from Moreno. "She needs to go to a hospital."

"I can stand now," Kat said.

Joaquin lowered her gently, keeping an arm around her shoulders.

Phone still held to his ear, Moreno studied Kat, then pointed to Joaquin. "Is he your husband?"

Kat shook her head, her face flushed, one hand pressed against her belly. "My husband isn't here."

"I remember." Moreno's expression changed, a subtle shift that sent a pulse of warning up Holly's spine. "Your husband must be the paramedic, yes?"

Kat's chin went up. "Yes."

Moreno walked a few paces and spoke into the phone once more, his lips curving into a hard smile. "She stays."

A collective gasp filled the room.

"What?" Joaquin took a step toward Moreno, began cursing at him in Spanish.

But Moreno turned his back on them all. "Tell her husband that her suffering is on *his* head."

Kat slumped against Joaquin, another contraction starting.

Holly turned away, sure her rage would show on her face. Reece stood there, fists clenched, helpless fury in his eyes. She lowered her voice to a whisper. "Next time he tries to drag me away, *don't* stop him."

21:18

TESSA ROCKED LITTLE ADDY, who'd woken up crying with a fever and earache. Laura Nilsson was on the screen, the sound down low. Tessa had given Addy some children's Tylenol and wrapped her in a lap quilt to keep her warm.

The four-year-old looked up at her through big blue eyes, little tears on her flushed cheeks. "I want Mommy."

God, what was Tessa supposed to say?

She stroked Addy's silky strawberry-blond hair. "I know, sweetie."

Up on the screen, Laura was reporting that the wounded who'd been evacuated from the Palace were expected to recover.

Thank God.

"Where's my Hoppy?"

Tessa glanced around, found him on the sofa. Hoppy was Addy's stuffed bunny. A little worse for the wear, he'd recently been stitched up and bravely wore a Disney princess Band-Aid on one foot.

"Hoppy is right here." She reached for him, tucked him inside the blanket with Addy, and went back to rocking.

Her cell phone buzzed.

Julian.

"Hey," he said.

"Hey. Any news?"

"Kat has gone into labor, and the bastard won't let her go."

"What?" Tessa's stomach knotted. "How far along is she?"

"She's at least a month early from what I've heard."

Damn it!

"Why wouldn't he let her go?"

"Because he's a fucking murdering asshole who needs a bullet through his ..." Julian drew a breath. "I'm sorry. I just ... "

"You don't have to apologize." She'd been hoping Moreno would catch a bullet from the moment she'd heard he'd struck Kara.

"How are things there? Are the kids still asleep?"

"Addy woke up with a fever. I think she has an ear infection. I've given her some children's Tylenol. I guess I'll take her to our pediatrician tomorrow if ... "

She couldn't finish the thought.

"Ah, hell. The poor little thing. I'm sorry. We'll get Hunter and Sophie out. Andris and Tower are inside with Hunter now. They called in to say he's okay."

Thank God for that.

"Are they going to be working with you all?" Tessa wanted to ask what their plan was to rescue everyone, but she knew he couldn't tell her.

"I'm not sure yet. I'm hoping they can help us figure out what we're facing—how many men, what kind of explosives, that sort of thing. The text messages I translated kept referring to a Christmas present in the basement. We need to find out what it is and whether it poses any threat to the hostages. How the hell they got all of this shit inside the hotel is anyone's guess."

"The tunnels." Tessa's heart skipped a beat. "I bet they came in through the tunnels."

Silence.

"Tunnels?"

"I wrote an article about them a long time ago, part of a 'Secrets of Denver' series." Tessa tried to remember the details. "There are two—a more modern one that dates to Prohibition that was used to move booze and coal into the hotel. It connects to the State Capitol building somehow. There's also an older one that was once used by hotel patrons to get to a brothel that was across the street without being seen."

"Jesus! How did you find out about them?"

"An old security guard at the Capitol told me. I'm sure not the only reporter who's written about them. It wouldn't be hard for anyone looking into the hotel's history to find out about them."

"God, I love you." He sounded better now, energized. "HRT is here. We're about ready to go into a briefing."

Her stomach sank, and she knew now why he'd called. "You're going in."

"I've gotten a tentative okay to join HRT."

"Oh." She tried to keep it light, not wanting to burden him with her fears and her emotions, not when he needed his mind focused on his job.

It felt like everyone she loved was in mortal peril tonight.

"If it were the two of us in there—"

"You don't need to explain. I understand."

"You are my life, Tessa. I'm going to do everything I can to get out alive and bring everyone else with me. I'll be working with the best of the best. I hope that gives you some peace of mind."

It didn't, not really. But she didn't say that.

"I know you'll do everything you can." Tessa fought back her tears. She wouldn't send him off with sorrow. "I love you, Julian."

His voice was soft. "I love you, too."

They disconnected without saying goodbye.

She fought back a sob, not wanting to wake the sick little girl in her arms.

God, watch over him. Watch over them all.

21:45

JULIAN STOOD IN THE back of the command center while Supervisory Special Agent Matt DeLuca, HRT's commander, introduced the team to Dixon and Irving. "SA Jake Evers, SA Sawyer Vance, SA Clay Bauer, SA Adam Blackwell, SA Ethan Cruz, SA Nathan Schroder. That guy is SA Brad Tucker, leader of Blue Team."

Tucker waved. "Call me 'Tuck.'"

The men acknowledged Dixon, Irving, and Julian with a nod or a wave of the hand, most of them wearing a day's growth of stubble on their jaws. All were former special operations forces—Navy SEALs, Delta Force, Marines Special Operations, Army Rangers, Green Berets—and together constituted the best-trained counterterrorist group inside the United States.

Julian felt a flash of savage satisfaction at what lay ahead for Moreno.

DeLuca crossed his arms over his chest and leaned back against the counter, a row of computers behind him, viewscreens above his head. "We've just come from an operation in Louisiana, but we've been getting regular updates from SA Dixon. We understand you've got something new."

Chief Irving nodded. "This is Detective Julian Darcangelo. I stole him from the Bureau a few years back. He used to work deep cover on child sex trafficking cases. He learned something you'll find interesting."

Julian stepped forward and pointed a remote at the big viewscreen on the back wall, where a street map of the neighborhood surrounding the Palace Hotel appeared.

"Moreno and his men got weapons and ordinance inside through a tunnel built back in 1922 to help move coal and contraband into the hotel. The tunnel is lighted and leads directly to the hotel's basement." Julian pointed to another screen, where a live feed from a street cam was running. "This shows Sherman Street in front of the State Capitol. Moreno and his men gained entry to the tunnel by posing as a repair crew and going in through a manhole. This is live. As you can see, he left a crew in place.

"They're probably there to cover his escape," Bauer said.

"Has anyone approached them?" DeLuca asked.

Irving shook his head. "We didn't want to give away the fact that we're onto the tunnel. And here's why."

Julian pushed a button on the remote, and a new image appeared on the screen. "There's an older tunnel that was built in the 1880s for hotel patrons who wanted to visit the brothel across the street without being seen."

"Illegal booze and brothels," Tucker said in a southern drawl. "Classy hotel."

"That brothel is now a bank. As you can see, that tunnel runs parallel to the main one. It's still there, though it's been sealed off on both ends. From what we've been able to learn, it's possible to access it through the crawl space beneath the bank."

"That's good work, detective," DeLuca said.

"Thank my wife," Julian said. "She's an investigative reporter."

"What's this we heard about guys on the inside?" Evers asked.

"My SWAT captain, Marc Hunter, was at a Christmas party with his wife in the hotel when the shooting started," Irving said. "He got away and took out four men on the roof who were setting up a Browning M2. They also had a Russian RPG-7."

Low whistles.

"Damn!" someone said.

"Hunter's still inside, together with two men from Cobra."

"How did Cobra come into this?" DeLuca asked.

Dixon got to his feet.

Jesus, could he give it a rest?

"They took an MH-6 to the rooftop in defiance of my orders, sir. I told them to stand down but—"

Julian cut him off. "The wife of one of their operatives is a hostage and was reportedly wounded in the initial firefight. She's an operative herself. Her special skill involves gathering intel through close personal contact. We don't know how badly injured she is, but she could be a resource for us."

Tuck snorted. "You know what this tells me?"

"What, man?" Evers asked.

"Moreno took the wrong damn bunch hostage."

DeLuca nodded. "So we have four people on the inside."

"Five," Irving answered. "The fifth is a former park ranger whose wife is also a hostage. She's pregnant and has gone into premature labor. Dixon tried to negotiate her release, but Moreno refused to let her go."

The men's expressions turned dark.

"Sick son of a bitch," DeLuca muttered under his breath, his brow folding in a frown. "I say we work with the Cobra guys and your SWAT captain, Irving. Have we established coms with any of them?"

Dixon nodded. "They are patched into our system."

"Have they gotten eyes on this 'Christmas present' in the basement?"

Julian shook his head. "No, sir, but we're assuming it's explosives—Moreno's insurance plan in case we try to mount a rescue."

One touch of a button, and the hotel could be blown to bits.

Tucker stepped forward, pointed to the older tunnel. "We could take Blue Team in here to locate and neutralize the 'Christmas present' and any tangos we find, while the Cobra team gathers intel on Moreno and his men—numbers, how they're deployed, any booby traps and so on."

Julian liked this idea. "Hunter counted at least twenty-four men working in teams of four or five. He and Rossiter have taken seven out of play—five on the rooftop and two in the loading dock. We've got their cell phones and have been answering their text messages, so Moreno doesn't know they're dead."

"Clever," Cruz said. "But sooner or later, he's going to find the bodies."

Julian nodded. "Either that, or he'll want to talk to one of them in person. When he figures it out, he might assume a rescue is underway and start killing people."

For a moment, no one spoke, the magnitude of the situation clear. But this was what they'd all trained for—Denver SWAT, FBI SWAT, HRT.

"We've got a bad situation here with a lot of lives at stake, including our Secretary of State and an unborn baby. What we *don't* have is time," DeLuca said, making eye contact with each member of Blue Team. "I want a rescue plan in place in fifteen minutes."

CHAPTER TEN

21:54

Tessa sat on the couch, doing her best to answer Tuck's questions over the phone, stroking Addy's hair, her heart breaking for the little girl. "Yes, sir, I toured them in person. I entered the newer tunnel through the basement of the State Capitol building."

"Were there side tunnels or other entrances along the way?"

"Not that I can recall. There were a lot of rats. We walked in what seemed like a straight line, stopping at a door that opened into the hotel's basement. They said it was just below the Grand Ballroom. There was a staircase that went up from there."

"That's very helpful," Tuck's tone of voice was soothing, his southern drawl comforting. "Did you enter the other tunnel, the older one?"

"No. It was more like a dirt tunnel, like a mine shaft. There were no electric lights. Some of the wooden supports were rotten, and they didn't think it was safe." After seeing the rats, Tessa had been pretty sure the older tunnel held even worse things and hadn't even asked to enter.

"Were you able to look into the older tunnel while standing in the other one?"

"Yes, sir. There was a place where the wooden supports and the concrete had crumbled. It was wide enough to step through." She'd found it both fascinating and creepy. "The concrete was pretty weak. I accidentally bumped it, and more of the wall fell away."

"That's great to know."

Addy sat up, rubbed her ear, Hoppy clutched to her chin, tears running down her little cheeks.

"It sounds like you have an unhappy little one there."

"She's got a fever, and her ear hurts. I think she's got an ear infection. She's Marc and Sophie Hunter's 4-year-old daughter. I'm watching their kids tonight. They're like family to us and ... " A hard lump formed in her throat, stopped her from saying more.

"Marc Hunter—the SWAT captain?"

She swallowed, blinked back her tears. "Yes, sir. His wife Sophie is ... "

Tuck finished for Tessa. "She's one of the hostages."

"Yes." Tessa was grateful she didn't have to explain further.

"If you'd like, I can send our team medic over. Nathan Schroder is a former PJ—pararescue jumper. He's the best. I'll tell him what's up. I think he has time to make a quick house call."

Tessa was astonished. "You ... you can do that?"

"Absolutely. You've been a big help tonight. I know Hunter has more than done his part, too. We take care of our own."

That was something Julian might have said.

"Thank you, Tuck."

"You got it. I'll get your address from your husband and send Schroder over."

The call ended.

Tessa held Addy close. "A doctor is coming to make you feel better."

"I want Mommy."

"I know you do, sweetheart. I know."

21:50

GARMENT BAG SLUNG OVER his shoulder, Zach bent low and hurried through the darkness toward the red brick building that served as the entrance to the United States Penitentiary Administrative Maximum Facility, or ADX for short—also known as Supermax or The Alcatraz of the Rockies. Dirt and pebbles kicked up by the rotor wash stung his skin, the ground dry as a bone. The prison warden, Ron Headley, greeted Zach and offered him coffee and a Danish.

"No, thanks. I need to get airborne with the prisoner as soon as possible."

"I understand." Headley moved with him through several levels of security toward a steel holding cell inside the prison itself, where Ortíz stood, shouting words no one could hear at guards he couldn't see.

"He doesn't know?"

"No, sir. We've done exactly what you requested."

Zach hadn't wanted to let Ortíz know why he was getting out, not until they were airborne. He wanted to do whatever he could to prevent word from spreading through the prison about Moreno and the hostage situation. He didn't want anyone getting ideas. "Open it up."

Ortíz looked surprised to see him. "You?"

Zach threw the garment bag at his chest. "Me."

Zach had been part of the team that had transported Ortíz to ADX after his sentencing.

Ortíz caught the bag. "What's goin' on, man? You can't just drag me around. You got to tell me what's up."

"Tonight is your lucky night, Ortíz. You're leaving."

Ortíz glared at him, angry. "Nah, man. Don't try to fool me."

Zach gave a snort. "You don't want out? That's okay by me."

He turned to go.

"Wait!" Ortíz called after him. "You serious, man?"

"I'm serious, man."

"What... ? Why... ?"

"Let's just say your cousin brokered a deal for you." Zach pointed to the garment bag. "Get out of the prison jumpsuit, and put on the pretty clothes. There's a helicopter waiting to take us to where your cousin in Denver."

Disbelief on his face, Ortíz opened the garment bag, saw the suit. "Nice threads."

"Yeah. Nothing but the best." One of the other DUSMs had grabbed them out of his own closet.

"You gonna leave me to dress?"

"No. You're going to strip naked and dress right here, right in front of me." Zach didn't want the bastard bringing any homemade weapons into the helo. None of the officers on this op were armed. They couldn't risk Ortíz stealing a firearm. That meant they needed to be extra cautious when it came to protecting themselves.

"*Malparido gonorrea*," he hissed at Zach. "You can't bust me for nothin' now that I'm leaving, right?"

"Me? No. I can't bust you for nothing."

A small blade of sharpened plastic fell from the waistband of Ortíz's underwear, hit the floor, bounced.

Zach stepped on it, slid it away from Ortíz and kicked it over to one of the correctional officers.

Ortíz stood naked, fumbling with the zipper on the trousers. "Quit staring at me. Stupid *maricón*. Fag. I bet you like to take it in the ass."

"Shut up, Ortíz." Zach put just enough authority in his voice to remind Ortíz what had happened during their last encounter.

The smirk left Ortíz's face. He slipped into the boxers, trousers, and dress shirt, and then held up the vest. "What's this?"

"Special body armor. Not everyone likes you as much as I do. It's part of my job to keep you safe."

Ortíz put it on, and Zach helped him strap it into place. "I'm really leaving?"

"Yes, really." He would also be coming back, but Zach didn't explain that part.

Ortíz was going to help save lives tonight, whether he wanted to or not.

The bastard slipped into the suit jacket, then put on the socks and the polished shoes, smiling up at Zach with a "fuck you" look in his eyes. "I knew Pepe would find a way to get me outa here. Man, I hate this place. It's evil. You got no idea."

"Cry me a river." Zach didn't feel like listening to more. "Let's go."

They were escorted back through security to the front entrance, a half dozen COs armed only with batons and stun guns on hand to ensure Ortíz didn't bolt. Then again, where would he run? It was pitch black and freezing out there, and ADX was in the middle of freaking nowhere.

At the doors, Ortíz balked, his gaze shifting from the darkness to Zach. "How do I know you're not taking me somewhere to kill me?"

"If I wanted to kill you, I would just do it right here and save myself time. Now either get with the program, or go back to your cell."

"It's cold. Don't I get a jacket?"

They had decided not to give him winter clothing in case he got away. Hypothermia could stop a man as surely as a bullet.

"Toughen up, cupcake." Zach gave him a shove.

Ortíz tripped out the doors and into the darkness, his anger with Zach vanishing the moment he saw the stars, a look of amazement coming over his face.

Enjoy it while you can, you son of a bitch.

Zach and his hand-picked team of DUSMs escorted Ortíz to the helo, helped him strap into his seat, three sitting behind, Zach sitting beside him just behind the pilot.

The helo's rotors started up, gained speed, the little craft rising off the ground, then nosing toward Colorado Springs.

Zach held fast to the remote in his pocket, leaned forward to speak rehearsed lines to the pilot. "Take the fastest route to Denver."

Ortíz let out a shout, looked back down at ADX, cursing it in Spanish.

"Excited?" Zach took out the encrypted cell phone the FBI had given him for this mission. "Tell your cousin all about it."

22:00

PEPE WAS TIRED OF talking. He'd been on the phone with Kimble, the new hotshot negotiator, for an hour. The *pendejo* was trying to ingratiate himself, trying to pretend like he cared what happened to Pepe and his friends. All he cared about were the hostages.

"We need to talk about the helicopter, too. Have you given any thought to what kind of helicopter you'll need? Your cousin will be flying into the city in a Blackhawk. They can carry up to fourteen men, plus the flight crew. Depending on how many men you plan to take with you, you might need something bigger. We have Chinooks on base at Fort Carson. They can carry up to forty-six."

Pepe wasn't going to leave in a helicopter at all. He was going to leave via the tunnel, and then blow the hotel sky high with the journalists, Sheridan, and that bitch Holmes still inside, but he couldn't say this. "The Blackhawk is fine."

"Okay. Good. We'll get you a Blackhawk."

They'd get him anything he asked for right now because he had the Secretary of State. He could have fun with this—make a few outrageous requests, laugh at their stupidity, watch them kiss his ass. But he didn't have the patience for it. The man's bland voice was beginning to fray his nerves.

"Do you have a pilot, or will you need a pilot?"

Pepe snapped. "Of course we will need a pilot!"

"Okay. That's good to know. Have you thought about other things you might want—clothes, food, maybe medical supplies?"

And it hit Pepe.

They were fishing. They were trying to get information.

The question about the helicopter was a way of forcing him to reveal how many men he had, the question about supplies a sneaky way of trying to find out if any of his men had been injured.

"Enough bullshit!" He was about to disconnect the call. "Don't call me again until my cousin—"

"Commander Moreno, I've just received word that your cousin is airborne. We're patching him through. Are you there?"

"Pepe?" Oscar's voice came over the phone.

Pepe found himself on his feet, adrenaline rushing to his head. He switched into Spanish. "Where are you?"

"I'm wearing a suit and sitting in a helicopter flying toward Denver." Oscar laughed. "You found a way, Pepe. I knew you would."

"Are you really in a helicopter?"

"*¡Sí!*" Oscar laughed again. "I can't believe it myself. Is it true you took hostages?"

Pepe's mind raced, searching for any way this could be a deception. "What do you see outside?"

"It's mostly dark, but there are city lights in the distance."

His plan had worked. The US government had buckled.

Of course it had worked. Pepe had known it would. He'd taken his time, thought of everything. Now his uncle would not be able to deny him his rightful place in the family business. He would be the favored nephew, equal to Oscar, the stupid *pendejo*.

"Ask the pilot how long it will be before you arrive." He waited on the line while Oscar asked.

"He says about two hours."

About two hours.

"That's cutting it close to the deadline I gave them."

"I'm so glad to be out of that place. It was terrible, Pepe. You are always alone—no sunlight, no one to talk to, just the thoughts in your head. I would rather be dead than live in such a place."

Oscar had always been weak.

Embarrassed for him, Pepe changed the subject. "We'll live like kings back in Colombia. Call me again when they say you're about to land."

"I will. *Gracias, mi primo.*" *Thank you, cousin.*

Pepe hung up the phone, a sense of triumph swelling behind his breastbone. He turned to his men, called out the news to them. "Oscar is free and on his way."

His men cheered, smiles on their faces.

"Well done, commander!"

He basked in their adulation, pulled out his phone, sent text messages to Luis and Camilo. He asked Camilo to take his place for a few minutes. All of this had gotten him riled up, made him horny. He wanted to spend some time with that little *puta*.

He motioned to her to come over.

The phone rang again.

"Commander Moreno, we're keeping our word. We need some reassurance from you, that you will keep yours."

Mother of God, he was sick of talking to this bastard. "The Moreno family is not the one that broke the agreement. The US government did that."

"You're working with me this time. I'm not the judge or the prosecutor. It's my job to make sure this turns out well."

"What do you want?" Even as Pepe asked, he knew. The pregnant woman. "I'm not letting anyone else go until my cousin and the thirty-five million are here."

"We've got a kit of supplies our medic put together for Kat James— things she'll need for herself and the baby in case she delivers before she's released. There are scissors for cutting the umbilical cord, a cord clamp, an injection of oxytocin to help prevent postpartum hemorrhage, as well as sanitary napkins."

Pepe's stomach turned at the description of the kit's contents, the idea of blood and gore coming out of a woman's body *there* sickening. "I will allow this. You can bring it to the loading dock."

"We've already left the kit on the fire escape outside the Onyx Room."

Pepe didn't like this. "I didn't say you could come up to the hotel."

Why hadn't the guys on the ground floor seen anything?

"You've got a woman in premature labor. Her life and that of her baby are on the line. You've gained the respect of a lot of our team out here, but you're going to lose all that if anything happens to mother or baby."

Pepe didn't give a damn about earning the respect of gringos—except that some part of him did. "I'll send one of my men for the kit, but this better not be a trick."

"I give you my word," said Kimble. "One of the hostages—Holly Andris—has some training as a nurse. She'll know what to do with it."

Pepe disconnected. "You didn't tell me you were a nurse."

She looked up at him, shrugged. "Well, I'm not a very good one."

Pepe couldn't help it. He laughed.

22:01

GABE ADJUSTED HIS HEADLAMP, listening while Tower went over the plan. He'd gotten a text from Chief Irving on the cell phone he'd taken telling him to meet Hunter, Andris, and Tower on the eighth floor, where they were waiting for him with a bag of gear. They'd brought him up to date, explaining that HRT was now calling the shots and outlining the plan.

Two would take up positions on the third floor that gave them unbroken lines of sight to the mezzanine balcony and the main doorway of the Grand Ballroom, ready to open fire on HRT's command. Someone else would stay on the roof to prevent Moreno's men from taking it back. Someone would make his way down the ventilation shaft to the floor above the Grand Ballroom—a mechanical floor filled with machinery and other equipment—where he would insert a slender camera through the ceiling so that guys in the command center could get eyes on both Moreno and the hostages.

Gabe had immediately volunteered for the latter. It fit his skill set, and he'd be as close as he could be to Kat.

Tower ran his finger over the image of the building plans on his tablet. "It's a six-story drop, and we don't know how snug it's going to get, what conditions you'll encounter, or what shape the metal is in. This hotel has been around since Custer was a child, so you might come across a clusterfuck of electrical wires or maybe pipes carrying hot water. Don't get yourself burned or killed. If you get stuck, we'll get you out when this is over. If you fall …"

"I won't fall."

"He won't," Hunter said. "Trust me."

Gabe gave Hunter a nod, appreciating the vote of confidence.

"Once you get there, look for hatches in the floor. Staff use them to service the lights in the Grand Ballroom. Look for an opening—it doesn't take much—to slide the lens of the camera through the ceiling. It should give HRT a view of the entire space. Listen to HRT's directions from there."

"Got it."

"And Rossiter?" Hunter said.

"Yeah?"

"Be quiet. If they hear you moving around up there …"

Wearing climbing shoes on his feet, Gabe lifted himself into the ventilation shaft, gear strapped to his chest in a small pack, his headlamp lighting the way.

It was easy going at first. He chimneyed his way down, using opposing pressure with his hands, knees, feet, and back on the sidewalls to control his descent, looking downward to make certain before he moved that the shaft walls weren't about to run out or change direction.

"How's it going in there?" Tower's voice sounded in his ear.

"It's like big-crack climbing in Moab or Yosemite."

Except dustier. And not at all scenic.

He must have gone down a good three or four floors when the shaft narrowed, making it almost impossible to look down. He was forced to climb back up to a wider space, remove his pack and tie it around the ankle of his prosthetic leg, and descend again, the metal pressed against his chest. It was a damned good thing he wasn't claustrophobic.

He was starting to worry that it would become so narrow that he would get stuck and wouldn't be able to breathe, when the pack hanging from his foot struck bottom. From there, it divided into four separate shafts, dropping at an angle.

"I'm at an intersection here."

"Take the one that heads north," Tower said.

"Right." Gabe shifted so that he could see his watch, which had a built-in compass, then slid into the shaft that headed in the direction closest to north, stirring up dust as he moved.

The shaft was almost horizontal now, enabling him to head down face first, but the metal was thinner here. It creaked and popped as he moved, raising the real possibility that someone would hear him. Dust tickled his nose, his throat, and he found himself fighting not to sneeze. "Are there any tangos near my position?"

"Negative," came the reply from the mobile command center.

Then Gabe saw light. It filtered through a small screen. Beyond the screen, he could see a room full of machines—furnaces, electrical panels, AC controls. He opened his bag, took out the hand drill, and removed the bolts holding the cover in place one by one, then held fast to the screen as he worked his way out of the shaft and lowered his feet to the floor.

"I'm in. Looking for those hatches."

Almost immediately he found them. Like small cellar doors, they opened on ordinary hinges. He chose one close to the place where they wanted him to insert the camera, opening it slowly to reveal the reverse side of a suspended ceiling—metal support beams, electrical wires, the back side of light fixtures. He took the snake camera out of his gear bag and lowered himself to one of the support beams. He found a spot where one of the fiberglass tiles had broken along the edge and pushed the lens of the camera through.

And then he heard it—the moans of a woman in pain.

The sound hit him in the sternum, made his chest constrict.

Kat.

CHAPTER ELEVEN

22:30

K at tried to relax, fought not to moan, but the pain was so intense it drove every conscious thought from her mind. She squeezed Joaquin's and Sophie's hands, looking into Sophie's eyes as the contraction peaked, held onto her as if it were trying to break her, then slowly ebbed.

"We've got you," Joaquin said softly.

Sophie pressed a cool, wet napkin to her forehead. "You're doing great."

That's not how Kat felt. She knew having a baby hurt a lot, but this was different. "The pain is so much worse this time."

It scared her.

What if something was wrong?

"You're early." Sophie's tone of voice was soft, soothing. "Your body probably wasn't ready for this. Being tense can make it more painful, too."

Kat knew this, and she'd tried not to tense up. But every time she opened her eyes, she saw men with guns and blood on the walls.

"I don't want them to hurt my baby."

Joaquin gave her hand a squeeze. "We're *not* going to let that happen."

Tears filled her eyes. "I wish I were on the dinétah."

Both Alissa and Nakai had been born on the Navajo reservation in a clinic about an hour's drive from her grandmother's homesite. She'd felt safe there, surrounded by Gabe's love and strengthened by her grandmother's reassurances and prayers.

Sophie stroked her hair. "Maybe if you pretended you were home it would help."

Kat's temper flashed. "How can I do that lying on this floor surrounded by men with guns?"

And then it hit her.

Hwéeldi.

The Long Walk.

All Diné people knew the story. The US Army had forced the Navajo to leave their homes and walk 300 miles to captivity at Bosque Redondo, a place they called Fort Sumner. Many Diné had died along the way of exhaustion, thirst, starvation, disease. Grandma Alice's great-grandmother had survived the Long Walk, but her great-grandmother's pregnant sister had not. She'd been shot and killed by a soldier when she'd gone into labor and stopped to give birth.

This wasn't the Long Walk, but Kat was a captive. Just like that soldier, her captors didn't care what became of her or her baby.

Another contraction began to build—and Kat began to sing quietly to herself. At first she wasn't even aware she was doing it, the words coming from somewhere inside her. Then she realized she was singing a traditional healing song, one she'd heard her uncle and grandfather sing when she was a little girl.

"Hamá hól□'□go 'ayóo jiníigo. 'Ayóo jiníigo t'áá bee hojílįį łeh ..."

As pain tightened its grip around her, the walls of the Grand Ballroom faded, becoming the red mesas that surrounded Grandma Alice's *hogaan* at K'ai'bii'tó. She latched onto the image of her home, felt Gabe standing there beside her, and Alissa and Nakai, too, the new baby out of her body and in her arms. Their spirits were together even if their bodies were not.

She thought of the young women who'd made the Long Walk, carrying babies on their hips or pregnant. She thought of another mother, one who'd lived long ago, who'd had no choice but to give birth in a pen for animals and place her newborn in a manger. Their strength became her strength.

Even after the contraction faded, she kept singing. Words had power, and the words of her people had come to her to help her through this.

She heard Holly's voice, knew Holly and Sophie were talking about the box of medical supplies the FBI had sent up. She let the voices drift over her, knowing that her friends were doing all they could to watch out for her and her baby. She pressed a hand to her abdomen.

It's going to be okay, little one.

22:33

"I'M SORRY, KAT. I have to pretend to be your nurse." Holly lifted the tiny GPS device from the roll of adhesive tape where the FBI guys had hidden it, not wanting to disturb Kat, who was singing softly to herself, her eyes closed, her cheeks flushed.

Kat gave an almost imperceptible nod of her head.

Holly took her wrist, pretending to take her pulse. She'd had advanced first-responder training and knew enough to be convincing.

Kat gripped Holly's hand, squeezed.

"Another contraction?" Holly asked.

Sophie nodded.

Kat's brow furrowed, her fingers all but crushing Holly's, but her singing didn't stop, even when the words became pained whimpers.

Damn Moreno! Damn him and his entire family!

The sight of Kat's suffering tore at Holly, bringing back her argument with Nick.

If we're going to have kids, we need to start soon.

That's easy for you to say. You're not the one who has to go through it. All you have to do is come.

I can't change human biology, but if you think I'd leave you to face it by yourself, you're wrong. I'm not that kind of man.

Holly's throat grew tight.

Oh, Nick.

Kat's grip on her hand lessened as the contraction came to an end.

Focus!

Holly released Kat's hand. "I'm going to do everything I can to help get us all out of here alive."

She stuck the GPS transmitter, which was no bigger than the active part of a SIM card, beneath the lace of her bra. She would put it on Pepe as soon as she got a chance.

How surreal this felt. She had spent years planting GPS devices and listening devices on suspected enemies of the United States. She'd never imagined she would be using that experience to try to save her friends' lives.

She'd already planted one listening device on the underside of the table where Secretary Holmes sat. Not even Secretary Holmes knew it was there. She didn't know about the GPS device Holly had hidden in the beading on the back of her gown, either. This second GPS transmitter was intended for Commander Asshat, who, as it turned out, was looking for her.

Holly's pulse spiked. She forced her fear aside.

You can do this.

She'd been in trouble before. She'd even killed before.

Pepe stopped walking the moment he saw Kat, turned his face away, snapping his fingers, motioning for Holly. "Come."

"I'll be back as soon as I can," Holly said to Kat, still playing nurse. Then she dropped her voice to a whisper, met Joaquin's gaze. "Don't interfere."

She stood, faced Pepe, let him see fear in her eyes. "She needs help. She—"

"Tell Camilo when he gets here that he is in charge until I return." He tossed his AK to one of his men, grabbed her wrist, and pulled her after him.

From around the room came jeers and whistles, Moreno's men cheering him on in what they assumed would be an act of rape.

"Stop! I'm not a whore!" Not that whores deserved to be raped, of course, but that was the best line Holly could come up with at the moment.

She pretended to struggle in the hallway, fought him when he tried to kiss her in the elevator, taking advantage of the opportunity to stick the GPS device on the underside of his collar.

He struck her cheek, pain rattling her brain, making her headache worse. "You think you can fight me, bitch?"

The elevator doors opened, and he jerked her out, pulling her down the hallway until he came to a room where the door had been left ajar.

He dragged her inside, flung her on the bed, and began to unzip his fly. "I'm going to fuck you so hard your pussy will be useless afterward."

Holly fought to master her pain and adrenaline. She had only one chance at this. There was no one to help her this time, no one listening in, no team ready to intervene.

"Please don't hurt me! I'll do whatever you want." She slipped the straps of her gown down her shoulder to expose her bra, then lay back and spread her legs, keeping them flat against the bed. "See? I'm ready for you."

He looked her up and down, his gaze fixing first on her cleavage and then her crotch, his lips twisting into a predatory smile. Then he yanked down her pantyhose and panties and tossed them aside.

Come and get it, you son of a bitch.

He clenched a fist in her hair, pulling hard, as he settled between her thighs. "I hope you like pain."

Holly brought her knee up, struck him hard in the groin.

He collapsed onto his side, coughed, moaned, his hands cupping his junk, his mouth open, his eyes wide.

"You said something about pain?" Holly pushed him off her, leaped from the bed, grabbed a curling iron from a nearby suitcase and wrapped the electrical cord around his neck once, twice, drawing it tight, putting all her weight into it.

His face turned red, his eyes bulging, fingers clawing at the cord.

"Jefe!" A shout came from the still open doorway.

Holly looked up, saw one of Moreno's men.

He rushed in, knocked her backward against the wall, took the cord from around Moreno's neck, speaking to him in Spanish.

Holly jumped to her feet, leaped onto the bed, hoping to reach the door.

Moreno's man grabbed her around the waist, threw her to the floor. She scrambled to her knees. His boot drove into her belly, pain driving the strength from her body and the breath from her lungs. Then a foot came down hard in the middle of her back, forcing her to flat onto the floor.

Moreno looked down at her, his face pale, one hand against his throat. "You ... fucking ... *bitch*."

And Holly knew she was dead.

22:47

PEPE SAT ON THE edge of the bed, afraid he would throw up, his breath coming in gasps, the pain in his balls radiating into his stomach and thighs. He struggled to his feet, wanting to kick her in the gut again and again, but he couldn't find the strength. "I'm going to kill you."

Tavo grabbed her by her hair, jerked her to her feet. "I came to tell you that Juandi is dead, and I cannot find Jhon. Also, Camilo has not come."

Pepe barely heard him, rage and pain consuming him. He'd been outdone by a woman, by a little *puta*. "You fucking bitch!"

He drove his fist into her stomach, watched her crumple. She was just a woman. Just a woman. How could she have gotten the better of him?

He looked up at Tavo. "The bitch almost killed me!"

"Jefe, you can deal with her later. Juandi is *dead*."

Tavo's words finally sank in.

"What do you mean Juandi is dead?"

"We found his body in the loading dock. He's been shot. There was a vial of cocaine on the floor next to him. Jhon was gone, and the door was wide open."

Alarm coursed through Pepe.

He'd known the *malparidos* with the FBI wouldn't keep their word. They had broken in. While he'd been distracted by this bitch, they had broken in and killed one of his men. Had they infiltrated the building?

He looked into the whore's face, saw defiance in her eyes. "When I get back, I'm going to make you suffer, and then I'm going to kill you."

She glared at him. "Go to hell."

"Tie her up. Make sure she can't get away. I'm going to find Camilo."

Pepe did his best to walk upright, pain still radiating through his groin. He pulled out his cell phone, called Camilo. The call went to voicemail.

This time, he called Luis. That call also went to voicemail.

Panic flared in his belly.

He called Yeison. "What the hell is going on?"

"Jefe? Everything is as it should be down here."

What did he mean by *down here*?

"Are you still in the basement? I told Camilo to send you and your men up to the roof to take over for Luis and his crew."

"I'm sorry, jefe, but I haven't heard from Camilo since you sent him to the roof."

What in the name of Satan …?

"Do you want me to go to the roof?"

"No. Stay where you are." Pepe would take Tavo and check it out for himself. "Muster your men. I want a head count."

He disconnected, retrieved his rifle, then went down to the loading dock with Tavo, where he found Juandi staring wide-eyed at the ceiling, two bullet holes in his chest, a vial of cocaine beside him, powder on his nose.

Jhon was nowhere to be found, the back door now closed.

Slowly, Pepe opened it, looked out into the alley.

No sign of Jhon. No sign of the FBI or SWAT.

Tavo spoke from behind him. "This casing is from an AK. SWAT and FBI don't use AKs. What if Jhon shot Juandi and then ran off?"

"Why would Jhon shoot Juandi?" Pepe's gaze darted to the cocaine.

Could drugs have anything to do with it?

Yeison called back. "Everyone is here and accounted for, *jefe*, but I still haven't seen Camilo or heard from him."

Pepe looked over at Tavo. "Come with me to the roof."

They took the service elevator up, then a long flight of stairs. The bulkhead door was open, frigid air spilling in. Weapon raised, he stepped out into the darkness—and saw no one. There was no sound apart from the wind.

Pepe made his way toward the place where Luis and his men were supposed to set up the machine gun, Tavo following behind him. Not only were the men missing, but the weapons were missing, too.

He turned slowly, chills that had nothing to do with the cold skittering up his spine, the roof giving a sniper a thousand places to hide. And then in the shadows he saw them—four bodies. He moved closer, needing to see faces.

Camilo and all of Luis's men. They'd been shot, spent AK shell casings scattered across the roof. But where was Luis?

"Jefe, here."

Pepe turned to find Tavo looking over the edge. Pepe stepped up to the parapets, glanced down, and saw a man's body splayed on the pavement below. He couldn't see the man's face, but he recognized the camo.

Luis.

But he'd just gotten a text message from Luis not ten minutes ago. Unless…

"Search for their cell phones!" he shouted to Tavo. "Do it!"

Tavo hurried over, searched the bodies. "They're gone."

How had this happened?

Pepe's mind raced.

It had to be SWAT. Those lying *hijueputas.*

But if they had taken the rooftop and the loading dock, why had they not rushed in on him and his men? Why would they kill a few of his men, abandon both places, and then disappear? How could they have reached the roof without being seen or heard? Where had the weapons gone? Who had been texting him?

It made no sense.

He looked to the northeast, saw what looked like Guillermo and his team still in position on Sherman Street, guarding their escape route, orange cones in the road. What if it wasn't Guillermo? What if the FBI had discovered the tunnel and replaced his men with special agents?

He called Guillermo and was relieved when he answered on the first ring. "Are all of your men accounted for?"

"*Sí, jefe.*"

Pepe let out a relieved breath. The tunnel was still their secret.

"Is there a problem?" Guillermo asked.

Pepe didn't want to look weak. "Stay sharp."

"Sí, jefe."

Pepe turned back toward the bulkhead, dialing Kimble's number.
"You stupid son of a bitch! I told you that if you sent a team in, I would
start killing hostages."

"We haven't sent anyone in, commander. I give you my word."

"Why are six of my men dead and one missing?"

"I think I might be able to help you unravel that mystery, but first I
need your promise that you won't hurt any of the hostages."

Why were they always asking *him* to make promises when they were
the ones who broke them?

"I promise nothing. *Nada.* Got that? Start talking, old man."

22:50

THEY MOVED SLOWLY AND deliberately through the darkness, Tuck in
the lead, Julian bringing up the rear just ahead of Bauer. Tuck had switched
his infrared headlamp to stealth mode as soon as they'd entered the tunnel,
giving their night vision goggles just enough light to function. Otherwise,
they'd be stumbling through pitch black.

The tunnel was exactly as Tessa had described it—like an old
mineshaft. Its floor, walls, and ceiling were made of dirt and were
reinforced by old timbers, many of which had rotted through and lay across
their path. They took care not to bump the walls for fear they'd collapse or
crumble and expose them to Moreno's men, whose muffled voices they
could hear on the other side of the wall.

The rats were there, too. Lots of them. The men stepped carefully around them, wanting to prevent the rodents from fleeing the tunnel in large enough numbers to alert Moreno's men to their presence.

In their earpieces, they all heard the news: Moreno had found his dead men and was threatening to kill hostages.

Time was growing short.

Ahead of him, Tuck stopped, turned off his infrared headlamp, dim light coming from a source ahead.

The breach in the wall that Tessa had described.

Tuck stopped, listened, watched—then stepped quickly past it.

One at a time, they moved to the other side of the opening, aware that being seen would likely mean their own deaths and the death of every hostage. Tuck, Evers, Blackwell, Schroder, Vance, Cruz.

Then it was Julian's turn.

He watched, waited, felt Bauer's hand on his shoulder. He was about to move, when footsteps stopped him.

One of Moreno's men appeared. AK slung over his shoulder, he made straight for the breach, stopping only feet away from Julian. He took his dick out of his pants and pissed into the darkness, urine pooling in the dirt inches away from Julian's feet.

Nice.

"Hey, *cabrón*, what are you doing?" someone called in Spanish.

"Taking a leak, man."

"Come on. Moreno said we need to stay sharp."

"I can't stay sharp if I never get to pee." The kid swore under his breath, shook off his dick, then shoved it back into his BDUs and hurried away.

Julian released the breath he'd been holding and hurried past the
breach, followed quickly by Bauer. They'd gone another twenty feet or so
when the tunnel came to a dead end. Tuck stopped and signaled to the team
to take up defensive positions. Julian knelt beside Bauer, weapon raised
and aimed back down the tunnel.

Behind them, Tuck worked with Evers to drill a small hole through
the wall and insert the tip of a camera. This was one of the riskiest parts of
the plan. If the concrete was too soft, the pressure of the drill might bring
the wall down, and they'd find themselves staring out at Moreno's men.
And wouldn't that just be awkward?

Julian knew they'd succeeded when DeLuca's voice sounded in his
earpiece.

"Good job, guys. We're getting a clear image, and ... Merry freaking
Christmas. It looks like they're trying to pull a McVeigh. There are a half-
dozen steel barrels that I'm betting hold fuel mixed with fertilizer. I'm also
seeing what looks like C4—probably meant to detonate the barrels.
There's easily enough explosives there to bring down the entire building."

Shit.

DeLuca went on. "There are a half-dozen men on the other side of that
wall, all armed with AKs, all looking up the stairs. None of them are
looking down the tunnel."

Well, that was their mistake.

Most of the time, SWAT and HRT tossed a few flash bang grenades
into a room to disorient the enemy before moving in. But they couldn't risk
detonating the explosives or giving away their presence to Moreno
upstairs. The perpetrator Rossiter had dumped naked in the alley had
spilled his guts when he'd regained consciousness and told the FBI that
Moreno had a remote detonator in his pocket.

One press of a button would end them all.

The plan from here depended on stealth. That's why they were all carrying suppressed MAC-10s loaded with subsonic 9mm rounds. They needed to take out the basement crew and disarm the explosive device—or ED—without alerting Moreno to their presence.

Tuck turned, and they followed him in order, heading back the way they'd come to the break in the wall. Julian felt Bauer's hand against his shoulder—a silent signal that he was ready. Julian reached forward, gave Cruz's shoulder a squeeze. And so it went up the line to Tuck. HRT was ready and in position.

Julian's muscles tensed for action.

Tucker stepped through the wall into the other tunnel, and the rest of them followed, moving as one toward Moreno's men and their "Christmas present." They came up silently behind them, took all six out with six suppressed shots, dropping them before they had time to react.

Julian searched the bodies, looking for cell phones, IDs, anything that might be a detonator, while Tuck and Bauer got down to work disarming the ED and the rest of the HRT guys secured the area, taking up defensive positions on the stairs and back down the tunnel.

"You ever seen anything like this?" Evers asked, kneeling down beside Tuck.

It was one hell of an impressive bomb.

"Yeah. We saw shit like this all the time in Iraq." Tuck sounded cool, almost casual. "Why? You nervous, farmboy?"

"You guys come here to talk or to work?" Bauer muttered.

Despite the gravity of their situation, Julian found himself grinning.

CHAPTER TWELVE

Nick watched the balcony through the scope of his M4, his gaze drawn again and again to the door of Room 335. If it was true that men made their own hell on earth, then he'd certainly found his.

He'd watched Pepe drag Holly into the room and shut the door, and he'd sat there and done nothing to help her, Hunter's voice in his earpiece, reassuring him that Holly knew what she was doing.

Of course, she did. She was resourceful, dangerously smart, and fierce as hell in her own way. She'd trained hard at close-quarters combat since joining Cobra, sparring with some of the best trainers in the business. She had surprised him on more than one occasion. Hell, she'd surprised everyone.

Still, Nick hadn't been able to lose the sick feeling in his stomach. He might have felt better about her chances if he hadn't had personal experience going up against her. She'd fought him hard, but Nick had gotten the upper hand.

Well, at least for a while.

A few minutes later, one of Moreno's men had stepped out of the elevator, rifle in hand, and had entered the room, and Nick's blood had gone cold. In a contest of Holly versus Moreno, he'd pick Holly. But Holly against two men?

He had promised DeLuca that he'd put HRT's objectives ahead of protecting his own wife. That had been the price he'd had to pay to work in tandem with HRT and not sit out the conflict on the sidelines. But watching that door shut, knowing Holly was alone with two killers, had made him regret that promise.

Yet, even in his desperation, he'd known he couldn't rush in to help her, not without risking the life of every hostage in the building. All Moreno had to do was push a button, and they would all die. He'd forced himself to stay where he was, their argument ringing through his head, filling him with regret.

Then the door to the room had opened again, and Moreno had stepped out, rubbing his throat and walking like he had a stick up his ass. He was followed several agonizing minutes later by his henchman. But there'd been no sign of Holly.

They'd been alone with her long enough to do whatever they'd wanted to do to her, long enough to...

No, he couldn't go there.

He couldn't help but go there.

If Moreno had hurt her—if he'd *raped* her—Nick would do whatever it took to help her heal. If she never wanted to have children, he'd be disappointed, but he'd adjust. Life without kids was one thing. But life without Holly ...

When will you be ready?

I don't know.

Yeah? Well, maybe you need to rethink your priorities.

He shouldn't have pushed her so hard. He shouldn't have let her walk away without working it out. God, he was a bastard!

Focus on the job, Andris.

Nick shifted his gaze back to the balcony, the chatter in his earpiece telling him that HRT had made it through the tunnel, taken out the bastards in the basement, and were hard at work defusing whatever explosives Moreno had stashed there.

One thing was certain.

Moreno and his men would not survive the night.

23:06

PEPE PACED THE BALLROOM, uncertainty leaving him itchy, making his palms sweat, fueling his rage. There was less than an hour to go to the deadline, and it was starting to unravel. His control was starting to unravel. That *puta de mierda* had crushed his balls and almost strangled him. Well, he could take care of her. But what was he supposed to do about his dead men?

He shouted into his phone. "You want me to believe that *one* man did all of this?"

"It's the truth." Kimble sounded so calm, so sure of himself.

"More government lies!" That's what his gut told him.

And yet his explanation was the only thing that put all the pieces together. The AK shells in the loading dock and on the roof. The white dress shirt on Gonzalo. The fact that SWAT hadn't yet put a bullet in his head.

"If SWAT had entered the building, you would know," Kimble reassured him, almost as if he could read Pepe's mind.

Pepe rubbed his aching throat. The slut had almost crushed his windpipe. He'd make her sorry soon. "You tell the bastard to turn himself over to me. If he won't, I'll pick six hostages and execute them to make up for the deaths of my men."

"I'm not in communication with him. I don't have—"

"You're the FBI!" Did they think Pepe was an imbecile? "If you know he's here, you must know who he is, and that means you can find a way to reach him."

"I understand that you're angry about what he's done, but you need to keep your eyes on the big picture here," Kimble advised him, his tone of voice patronizing. "Your cousin is on his way. Don't do anything to jeopardize your success here tonight."

Pepe stopped pacing, fury making his face hot. "Don't fuck with me! If you harm my cousin—"

"Oh, I'm not threatening him. No harm will come to your cousin—none at all," Kimble assured him. "However, if you start shooting hostages, you would be putting yourself and your men at risk."

That was a threat.

Did the *carechimba* not take him seriously?

Pepe spoke so that everyone in the ballroom could hear him. "If you go back on your word, if you try to rescue the hostages, they will *all* die."

Kimble didn't react to this at all, as if nothing Pepe said could shake him. Had Pepe lost his respect? "I heard you loud and clear the first time you said that, and we're willing to work with you—provided the hostages remain safe."

"Are you going to contact the bastard are not?"

"As I told you, we don't—"

"Go to hell." Pepe ended the call, glanced around at the terrified faces.

Mamagüevos. Malditas putas.

Cocksuckers. Fucking whores.

They could all fuck off and die.

Pepe needed to do something to regain Kimble's respect, something to show that he was in control, not the FBI, not Kimble, and certainly not this fucker who had killed his men. "Six of my men are dead, and the FBI won't give me the man who killed them. Tavo, pick six people, take them into the hall, and execute them."

When Tavo hesitated, Pepe grabbed the fat man who'd complained that he was having chest pain and dragged him toward the door. "Five, Tavo. Now!"

"What are you doing? Y-you can't kill me! I'm Charles Baird. I'm the newspaper's publisher!" The man tried to pull away, but he was weak and soft.

"In a moment, you will be nothing." Pepe locked his arm around the asshole's neck, hauled him toward the door, some of his itchiness fading.

"I can tell you who killed your men!" the man shouted, his voice high-pitched from fear. "I can tell you who he is! That's what you wanted from the FBI, right?"

Pepe stopped, released him. "How do you know this?"

The man looked up at him, his pale face sweaty. "His wife works for me."

"His wife?" Pepe found himself smiling. He didn't need help from the FBI if he had the whoreson's wife. "Who is she?"

The man turned and pointed. "Sophie Alton-Hunter."

At the sound of her name, a pretty woman with reddish-blond hair got to her feet and turned to face him, the fear in her eyes confirming the truth.

"Her husband is captain of Denver's SWAT team," the fat man offered. "He came to the party with her but disappeared when the shooting started."

Captain of Denver's SWAT team? That was something Kimble hadn't shared.

Pepe patted the man on his shoulder. "Your cowardice has saved your life."

Nearby, Tavo was dragging a screaming older woman toward the door.

"Let that one go, Tavo." Pepe pointed to the SWAT captain's wife. "Take her."

Tavo waded into the crowd and grabbed the woman, who, to her credit, did not scream or struggle.

"Take me!" shouted a man—the man who'd brought the slut. "She's a mother. She has two little children. Take me instead!"

"I'm sorry," Pepe told him, not feeling sorry at all. "You are of no importance."

Tavo brought the woman to stand before Pepe.

She looked boldly at him despite her fear, but said nothing.

"I remember you." Pepe smiled. "You arrived with a tall man with brown hair. You were laughing about something. Where is he—your husband?"

"I-I don't know."

He stroked her cheek. "I believe you. How could you know? You've been here, helping your pregnant friend, while he has been off killing my men. He left you behind and saved only himself."

Her chin came up at this insult, but she wisely said nothing.

"Tavo, hold your pistol to her head." Pepe slid out his cell phone. "I'm just going to take a little photo."

Tavo did as he asked, the redhead giving a little gasp when the barrel pressed against her temple. Pepe snapped the photo, then sent it in a text message to Kimble. Not even ten seconds had passed before his cell phone rang.

Pepe laughed to himself, the situation once again firmly in his grasp. He didn't give Kimble a chance to speak. "You didn't tell me the bastard killing my men was Denver's SWAT captain. As you can see, I have his wife. If he does not turn himself in to me, I will put a bullet through her pretty head. He has five minutes."

23:10

HOLLY TWISTED HER WRISTS, trying to loosen the bonds that held her arms behind her back and bound her to this chair. No way was she going to die because some freaking jackhole had tied her up with her own pantyhose. He'd put some effort into it, too, then told her in broken English that Moreno planned to strangle her just like she'd tried to strangle him— but only after he and his men had gotten tired of her.

Then the jerk had surprised her by offering to help her—if she would give him a blow job. She'd seen in his eyes that he was lying. But even if he'd been telling the truth, her answer would have been the same.

"If you stick your dick in my mouth," she'd said sweetly, "I'll bite it off."

That had earned her a slap across the face, but it had been worth it.

Did he think she was an idiot? She had no doubt Moreno would kill her. She'd done the unforgivable and gotten the better of him. She'd hurt him, humiliated him. Yes, he would kill her—but not before he'd made her suffer.

That's why she wasn't going to be here when he got back. Any second now, the knots that held her fast would give way, and she would get out of this room.

She stopped, rested her arms, panic starting to build in her belly.

"Hey, guys," she said to SWAT and HRT, "how about a rescue?"

They couldn't hear her, of course. The listening devices she'd received in the first aid package had all been planted in the Grand Ballroom.

She fumbled with her bonds again, trying to make the stretchy fabric yield just ... a ... little ... more... But the bastard had pulled all the stretch out of it, the nylon or whatever it was biting into her skin, cutting off her circulation.

Nick.

She had no idea where he was, no idea whether he and Cobra were involved in some way tonight. But she knew her husband. He wouldn't want to sit on the sidelines and watch. He'd do everything he could to get to her.

He loved her.

The thought brought tears to her eyes—and made her angry.

She was *not* going to die at the hands of Commander Asshat.

She rested again, then tried once more, wondering how a brand of pantyhose that always seemed to get runs when she needed them to look perfect could possibly withstand all this twisting and pulling when she needed them to tear. Clearly, it was time to switch to a different brand.

Damn it!

This wasn't working.

She decided to try breaking the wooden back of the chair. It was an antique, which meant it must be fragile, right? She dug her heels into the carpet and, pushing hard against it, moved from side to side and slammed it back against the wall.

Ouch!

She'd gotten her knuckles.

Next, she tried to stand, thinking she'd open the door with her head, then move as quickly as she could to another room, chair and all. It took a couple of tries, but she managed to get to her feet.

"Yes!"

She'd gone a couple of steps toward the door, when one of the legs hit the chest of drawers, throwing her off balance. She crashed to the floor, landing painfully on her side.

Freaking perfect!

She was about to try getting back on her feet again, when the door handle turned with a click. Adrenaline shot through her, but there was nowhere for her to go, no way for her to fight, nothing to do but survive whatever happened next.

And she *would* survive. She had so many reasons to live.

The door swung wide, and she found herself looking up not into Moreno's face, but that of the jackhole.

He smiled, chuckling to himself. "I make the knots tight, yes?"

In the next instant, a hand covered his face, and a knife slashed across his throat, his eyes bugging wide as blood spilled down his neck and onto his chest.

"Nick!"

He threw the man's body aside and stood there in full tactical gear, a rifle on his shoulder, the K-Bar knife still in his hand. He bent down, cut her bonds, then sheathed the blade, and helped her to her feet, his arms encircling her, drawing her tight against him. "God, Holly."

"Good ... timing ..." Holly squeezed the words past the lump in her throat, clinging to him, his body, or at least his body armor, hard against her.

"Are you okay? You look like hell." He glanced at the side of her head, touched a gloved finger to the bruise on her cheek, his gaze going hard. Then he saw something on the floor. He bent down, held up her panties. "Did he ... hurt you?"

She knew he wasn't just asking about bruises. "He didn't get time to do more than knock me around. I kneed him in the nuts."

The relief on Nick's face made warmth blossom in her chest.

He loved her. He still loved her, despite their fight. And she loved him.

"I'm so sorry—for everything." He glanced over his shoulder, pressed a finger to his hidden earpiece. "We need to get you out of here—now."

"Where is HRT?"

"In the basement, trying to defuse a bomb."

Oh, well, that explained a few things—such as why Moreno was still living and breathing and hurting people.

"Do you want to lie low, or do you want to be part of the takedown?"

"Are you kidding me?" She grabbed her panties out of his hand, stepped into them. "Give me a freaking weapon."

23:10

FIVE MINUTES.

Was that all that remained of Sophie's life with Marc?

She'd thought they still had a lifetime ahead of them. Watching Chase and Addy grow up. Proms. Weddings. Grandchildren. Gray hair. But unless SWAT raided the hotel in the next few minutes, one of them was going to die. And she was terribly afraid she knew which one of them it would be.

"How much does your husband love you?" Moreno asked the question with a smile, his tone of voice mocking, his cell phone buzzing in his pocket.

"You're despicable." The words were out before Sophie could stop them. "My husband is strong, brave, honorable—all the things you'll never be."

Moreno's smile faded, his upper lip curling. "Is he honorable enough to die for you? Would he give his life to save yours?"

Oh, yes, he would. He'd proven that years ago when he'd jumped in front of a bullet meant for her. He'd sacrificed his future for his sister and niece. He was in this situation tonight because he'd been trying to save lives.

Oh, Hunt.

But Sophie didn't answer Moreno. The bastard was excited by her fear, by the control he had over her, over all of them. If these were the last five minutes she had on this earth, she wouldn't spend them dancing on his string.

She turned away from him, her gaze seeking out Matt, who had just offered to die for her. He stood not far away, Alex still holding him back. She wished she could give him a hug. "Thank you."

"I'm sorry," he said, as if Moreno's unwillingness to kill him instead were somehow his fault.

Mr. Baird looked up at her, shrugged. "I didn't know he was going to do this. I ... I didn't know."

"Shut up!" Alex shouted at him. "You're pathetic."

Sophie willed herself to look into his eyes. She couldn't blame him for being afraid, for wanting to save his own life, but he had betrayed Marc to a killer. She said the kindest thing she could think of under the circumstances. "Don't ever speak to me again."

Her pulse was racing now, her heart thudding behind her breastbone, the minutes rushing by. Everyone in the room seemed to be staring at her.

Moreno's phone buzzed again. Still he refused to answer.

Sophie's gaze was drawn to the ballroom's doors.

"It doesn't look like he's coming."

Snickers from Moreno's men.

And some part of her began to hope.

Maybe he was no longer here and couldn't make it in time. Maybe SWAT was about to raid the place. Maybe he didn't know because the FBI truly couldn't reach him.

She didn't want to die. She didn't want Chase and Addy to grow up without her. But dying would be easier than facing every day of the rest of her life without Hunt.

Tears pricked her eyes. She blinked them back.

"Two minutes left." Moreno laughed. "Are you scared?"

Two minutes?

My God.

Her heart beat faster.

Sophie willed herself to smile. "Not for myself."

There was so much she wanted to say to Hunt, to Chase, to Addison, to her brother, to her friends.

"If you kill either of them, Moreno, you're going to bring a world of shit down on your head." Reece's voice brought Sophie's gaze to the other side of the room, where he and Kara stood together, holding hands, helplessness and anger in their eyes. "Answer your phone. Talk to Kimble. There has to be a better way to resolve this than killing an innocent woman."

Sophie gave Kara a smile, wishing she could tell her how much her friendship had meant over these past eleven years.

But Reece wasn't giving up. "She had nothing to do with your cousin being in prison. She's a mother of two little children, for God's sake. Do you have children?"

"Not that I know of." Moreno laughed, glancing around at his men, who laughed too. "One minute."

He motioned one of his men over to her, cold fingers grasping her arm, pulling her roughly toward the doors.

Sophie looked over her shoulder toward Matt, time running out. "Don't feel bad. Tell Marc not to blame himself. Tell him—"

"Tell me what?"

Marc!

Her heart gave a hard thud, then seemed to shatter.

She'd known he would come.

He stood just inside the ballroom door, shirtless and shoeless, duct tape stuck over a bloody wound on his rib cage, streaks of dried blood on his abdomen, his hands behind his head.

Tears filled her eyes. "I love you."

CHAPTER THIRTEEN

23:15

Marc saw the terror in Sophie's eyes and wanted to crush Moreno. He crossed the ballroom, came in between Sophie and Moreno, gave her a smile. "Sorry I'm late."

He hadn't meant to cut it so close. The moment he'd heard from DeLuca that Moreno was threatening to kill Sophie, he'd known his time was up. DeLuca had warned him that they wouldn't be able to protect him. They couldn't give themselves away until after the ED was defused. And Marc had understood.

He'd broken from the pack. He was on his own now.

But he wasn't going to endanger anyone else. To make the FBI's story work, Marc had stripped out of his tactical gear and stashed it somewhere the bastards wouldn't find it before making his way to the mezzanine level. If he'd shown up in SWAT gear, he'd have blown it for all of them.

Sophie's chin trembled. "I wish you hadn't come."

Something twisted in his chest.

He knew she meant it, but no way was he going to let a terrorist kill the woman he loved, the mother of his children. If Moreno wanted him, he could fucking have him.

"Not a chance." He reached out, slid a thumb over her cheek.

Marc needed to buy time—for himself, for Sophie, for HRT.

He locked down his emotions, turned to look down at Moreno, who was shorter than he was by a head—and had deep purple bruises around his throat, as if someone had tried to garrote him. Had Holly done that?

"You're not so big after all, Moreno."

"You're the *mamagüevo* who killed my men?"

"Yeah." Marc crowded him, forcing Moreno to take a step back. "They had no clue what they were doing up there. You'd think they had never assembled a machine gun before. Oh, wait ... You mean they hadn't?"

Moreno's nostrils flared, and Marc could see he was pissed. "What did you do with the weapons?"

"I disassembled them, threw some pieces over the side of the building, and hid the rest." He moved toward Moreno again, forcing him to step back once more, putting as much space as possible between him and Sophie.

One of Moreno's men stepped forward. "We should send him up there, hold a gun to his bitch's head, and force him to put the weapon together again."

"*¡Maldito idiota!*" Moreno turned on the man, who backed quickly away. "He threw some of it off the side of the building. Do you think we should also open the doors and let him walk about in the streets?"

Come on, HRT!

"I could try, if you'd like, but that's a lot of screws and shit to find in the dark."

Moreno glared up at him. "You killed my men, and now you're going to die."

Marc faked a Spanish accent. "'My name is Commander Moreno. You killed my men. Prepare to die.' You've watched too many movies if you think you can get away with killing a cop."

Moreno glared at him, his brow furrowed. "What are you saying?"

"*Princess Bride*. You mean you haven't seen ... ?" Marc raised his eyebrows, blew out a breath. "Wow. And, hey, man, what happened to your throat? You've got serious ring around the collar."

Moreno looked completely confused now. He rubbed his throat, then drew something out of his pocket. "What you said about not getting away with it—you're wrong. I have this."

Marc knew he was holding the detonator in his hand, but feigned ignorance. "A garage door opener? Or maybe you push the button, and it turns you into a real man."

Moreno glared at him, got right in his face—or his chest, really. "I push the button, and a bomb destroys this building and everyone in it. So don't fuck with me."

Gasps. Alarmed whispers. Crying.

Somewhere, a woman singing.

Kat. Poor Kat!

Marc raised a brow. "So if I fuck with you, you'll commit suicide?"

"And kill everyone in this building, including your whore."

Marc shook his head. "I don't know, man. How is that a victory? If I were you, I'd want to go home in one piece."

Moreno slid the detonator back into his pocket, jabbed Marc in the chest with a finger. "That is because *you* are a coward."

Marc crowded him again. "You hit and hurt defenseless women and hold more than three hundred people at gunpoint, one of them a woman about to have a baby, and *I'm* the coward? When I took on your men, I was outnumbered four to one, and *they* had the rifles. Tell me, Moreno—who's the coward?"

He saw in Moreno's eyes the moment he snapped.

The bastard stepped back, motioned to two of his men, his gaze locked with Marc's. "Take this piece of shit out into the hallway, make him get on his knees, and shoot him in the back of the head. If he resists, I'll shoot his bitch."

Marc turned to Sophie, took her into his arms, and held her tight, pressing a kiss against her hair. "It's going to be okay, sprite. You'll be okay."

Her voice was tight with tears. "I love you, Hunt. I am so proud of the man you are. Chase and Addy are going to grow up so proud of their father."

Marc caught her face between his palms, tilted it up toward his, kissed her on the mouth, his thumbs brushing her tears away. "You're everything to me."

Moreno's men jerked him away, Moreno laughing as they hauled him off.

Marc caught Reece's gaze. "Take care of her."

Already, Matt and Alex had come forward and now stood on either side of Sophie, who watched him, terror in her blue eyes, tears streaming down her face.

They turned him around, forced him back out the doors and onto the balcony. At least they weren't going to kill him in front of Sophie. He could be grateful for that. He caught one last glimpse of her over his shoulder—Sophie, his sprite.

"Down on your knees."

"Suck my dick." If he could just buy another few minutes...

One of them struck him in the back of the knees with the butt of a rifle, forcing him to kneel.

He'd thought he'd bluff his way out of this, fuck with Moreno's head long enough for HRT to make its move, or maybe fight his way out of it. But Sophie's life depended on his surrender, so he would surrender. For her sake, for the kids who needed their mother, for the woman he loved.

Images chased one another through his memory. Sophie at sweet sixteen, offering herself to him on a starry night in the desert. Sophie cuffed to a bed, his hostage. Sophie holding newborn Chase in her hands. Sophie making pancakes for him and the kids last Christmas morning. He'd had a good life. Because of her, he'd had a good life.

Behind him, someone racked the slide of a pistol.

Time's up, Hunter.

Marc had always known he would die in the line of duty. He just hadn't expected it to happen so soon.

God, watch over Sophie and the kids. Watch—

BAM!

23:18

JULIAN STOOD ON THE stairs, ready to move.

In his earpiece, he heard DeLuca's voice. "The situation upstairs is critical."

"Just a few more minutes," Tuck said. "This one?" He pointed at one wire in the tangled nest that was the ED's detonator.

"Yeah," Bauer answered. "No—this one."

"You sure?"

"Hell, yeah, I'm sure."

Someone had better be sure—and fast.

Ahead of Julian, Cruz shook his head, a grin on his face.

So the bickering was part of their EOD routine. Good to know.

Julian had gotten a few minutes to talk with Schroder, who'd made a house call with antibiotics and some eardrops for little Addy that he'd acquired from a nearby hospital pharmacy. He'd said Tessa was doing well and that her mother and step-father had come over to wait the night out with her. Julian had been grateful for Schroder's help—and glad to hear Tessa wasn't alone.

DeLuca spoke again. "They've taken Hunter out into the hallway to execute him. Andris, Tower, do *not* intervene, or you'll risk giving us all away. Copy."

"Copy that."

Son of a bitch!

And then...

"Live shooter. I say again, live shooter. We have a shot fired."

Julian felt like he'd been punched in the gut, breath rushing from his lungs.

Hunter.

It couldn't have been him. It couldn't have.

Jesus!

"You okay, buddy?" Cruz reached over, put a hand on Julian's shoulder.

Julian forced his emotions aside, willed himself to concentrate on the job. Sophie was still up there—and Kat. Sheridan and Kara. The rest of the newspaper staff. Not to mention Secretary Holmes. They were depending on him and the men of HRT to be professionals, to do the job they'd been trained to do.

Julian wouldn't let them down. "I'm fine."

If Hunter was dead, Julian would kick his ass.

FBI SWAT had come through the old tunnel and now stood ready to back up HRT on Tuck's command, a dozen men strapped and ready to play rough. The plan was to move silently up the stairs and into the service hallway, taking out the men Moreno had posted there without being heard. Then they would toss flash-bang grenades into the open area of the Grand Ballroom and rush in, taking out Moreno and his remaining men before they could open fire on the hostages. At the same time, DPD's SWAT— Hunter's team—would move in on the bastards on Sherman Street.

"That's it," Tuck said. "Device is deactivated. We're good to go."

Tuck and Bauer got to their feet, put their helmets back on, checked their gear. Then Tuck moved to the foremost position, his gaze meeting those of his men and then Julian's as he passed. "Let's get these bastards."

Tuck moved up the stairs like a ghost, the rest of his men and Julian falling in behind him, FBI SWAT taking up the rear.

23:19

HOLLY WATCHED MARC PITCH face-first onto the carpet, hands pressed against his ears, an expression of pain on his face. She lowered her voice to a whisper, her own ears ringing. "Sorry!"

Marc looked up at her, apparently surprised to discover he wasn't dead. He got to his feet, looked down at the two men who were, his gaze lifting to Holly's once more. "How'd you get two at the same time?"

Holly pointed to Nick, who stood out of sight behind one of the pillars.

Nick gave Marc a thumbs-up, then motioned to them to hurry up.

"Help me move them," Holly whispered. "I don't want Commander Asshat to look out and see them."

Marc nodded, grabbed one of the men and pulled him into the shadows, then came and took over for Holly, who'd managed to drag her dead guy only about half that distance. When both bodies were concealed, he confiscated a firearm, and the two of them made their way over to Nick.

"You know, you cut it close there," Marc said. "I thought I was a goner."

"Sorry, Hunter. I had to make sure not to hit you, or you would be."

Marc rubbed his ears. "I'm going to be deaf."

Nick grinned. "Hey, but you're alive."

"Yeah." His voice was calm, but Holly could see beyond the badass exterior to the emotions he was fighting to suppress—shock, relief, rage.

"I'm sorry about the noise." She tried to explain. "I had to take the suppressor off the pistol because those guys didn't have suppressors and—"

Nick cut her off. "Do you two think we can hold this little debriefing later?"

Holly nodded. "Right."

"I want the two of you out of the way when the action starts. Neither of you are in uniform or wearing body armor, and HRT doesn't know you're with me. I don't want to risk your becoming collateral damage."

Holly didn't like this. She *owed* Moreno. "What about this dress and these heels makes me look like a narco-terrorist?"

Nick didn't answer, but turned to Marc. "Watch over my wife?"

Marc nodded. "You'll watch over Sophie?"

Holly gaped at them. She'd just killed a bad guy, shot him at almost point-blank range in the side of the head. Why were they talking about her as if she weren't in the room? "Hey, I'm a grownup operative. I can take care of myself."

But they weren't listening.

"You got it, Hunter." Nick turned to go, but Marc had one more question.

"Does Sophie know?"

Holly shook her head, her heart hurting for her friend, who believed her husband had just been murdered.

A look of pure anguish came over Marc's face.

Nick clapped him on the shoulder. "It will be over soon."

23:19

GABE WATCHED THROUGH A gap in a ceiling tile as Sophie's knees gave out and she crumpled into Matt's arms, her grief hitting him in the solar plexus, mingling with his own shock and fury.

Jesus! Hunter.

Goddamn it!

Moreno laughed about something—the filthy son of a bitch—then started toward the door, saying something to one of his men about the "*puta de mierda.*" He was headed back to wherever he'd stashed Holly. Poor Holly.

Was DeLuca catching this? If Moreno disappeared before they moved in...

Well, that was HRT's problem.

Gabe's problem was protecting Kat.

Below him, she worked through another contraction, Joaquin holding her hands, doing his best to help. Gabe had watched for what felt like hours now, helpless to do anything for her, every contraction making his chest hurt. But he was done waiting.

He did a quick count of the men in the room. The two who'd murdered Hunter hadn't come back. One had disappeared some time ago—the one Moreno called Tavo. He hadn't come back either. That left Moreno and two others, and right now they weren't looking this way.

Gabe saw his chance and took it.

He checked his pistol and tucked it into its holster, then slid the ceiling tile aside, crouched down—and dropped twenty feet to the floor.

He landed beside Joaquin, who gave a startled jerk, then glared at him. "You *are* loco, man."

"Thanks, Joaquin." The man had been a rock for Kat, and Gabe wouldn't forget it.

But he was here now.

He moved to Kat's side, keeping his back to the rest of the room, not wanting anyone to recognize him. He'd seen what that bastard Baird had done to Marc and Sophie. He didn't want to risk the same thing happening with him and Kat.

She was singing softly, sweat beaded on her forehead, her hair damp. She didn't seem to know he was there.

He took one of her hands from Joaquin. "Kat, sweetheart, I'm here."

She opened her eyes, stared up at him, then threw her arms around his neck. "I thought you were gone. I thought you were safe."

"I never left. I've been up there, watching over you, for most of the time I've been away." He pointed up at the missing tile. "I'm sorry I left you."

"Not … your fault." She settled herself against him, her brow furrowing with pain, her hand tightening around his until her knuckles were white.

Not for the first time in his life, Gabe wished he could take this from her, even if for just a little while. Nature hadn't divided things evenly when it came to reproduction. All he could do was hold her, kiss her, tell her he loved her.

The contraction peaked, then slowly ebbed.

"It's different this time. The pain—it's so much more intense." She met his gaze, her eyes clouded by fear. "What if something's wrong with the baby?"

If he'd had any real medical gear with him, he might have been able to check for the baby's heartbeat to reassure her, but he didn't.

Then he heard Tuck in his earpiece.

He leaned in, whispered to Joaquin. "You should get Sophie, Matt, and Alex. Tell them to sit down. Keep it low key, casual."

Joaquin didn't hesitate.

Gabe brushed the hair out of Kat's face. "In a minute, they're going to toss flash-bang grenades into the room and take out the bad guys. There will be some big explosions and gunfire. Try not to let it scare you. You're safe now."

No one would touch her.

She nodded, closed her eyes, rested against him.

23:21

PEPE WALKED OUT OF the Grand Ballroom, his groin growing heavy at the thought of that little slut and her big brown eyes. At least he could still get a hard-on. She hadn't ruined him. He had a little while before his cousin arrived, and he intended to spend it using her, making her pay for what she'd tried to do to him.

Outside the doors, he stopped, glanced around him, the hair on the back of his neck rising. He had expected to see Diego and Héctor out here, standing over the SWAT captain's body. But they weren't here.

Neither was Hunter's corpse.

He called for them. "Diego? Héctor!"

No answer.

On the carpet, he saw two fresh trails of blood that led to...

Diego and Héctor.

They were dead.

Pepe drew his pistol, glanced around him. "Hunter! I still have your wife! You were going to die for her, remember, you coward? Now I will kill her! Nothing you can do now will save her!"

Heart pounding, his face hot with rage, he strode backward into the Grand Ballroom, his gaze seeking out Hunter's whore.

He saw her sitting near her pregnant friend again, three men sitting around her like guard dogs. He tried to remember her name. "Sophie Hunter!"

She turned her head to look at him, her eyes going wide.

He raised his pistol.

Bang! Bang! Bang! Bang! Bang!

Explosions went off around him, the blasts making him jump, smoke filling his eyes, his lungs.

Screams. Men's shouts. Gunfire.

¡Hijueputas!

His bowels turned to liquid, his heart pounding sickeningly in his chest, panic scattering his thoughts. Still, somehow he knew.

They were trying to free the hostages.

¡Dios mío! ¡Dios mío! ¡Dios mío!

Men swarmed over the room, weapons raised.

He jammed his hand into his pocket, drew out the detonator.

Something punched him in the chest. His legs turned to water beneath him, and he fell to the floor, pressure making it impossible to breathe.

He'd been shot!

Holy Mother of God!

The *hijueputas* had killed him. He was going to die. He and all his men were going to die. No, they were *all* going to die together—every last person here.

He looked over at his hand—strange that he couldn't feel it—and willed his thumb to push the button.

Nothing.

Someone kicked the device from his grasp, the spiky heel of a woman's shoe coming down on his palm, nailing his hand to the floor.

The little slut stood looking down at him, loathing in her eyes. "Enjoy hell, you son of a bitch."

He opened his mouth, but no words came out, only a gurgling sound.

And then...

Darkness.

CHAPTER FOURTEEN

23:30

Reece raised his head, saw that Moreno was dead, men in black tactical uniforms moving through the room. He sat, drew Kara up with him. "Are you okay?"

God knew she'd been through enough tonight.

She nodded, but then her brows drew together in a concerned frown. She pressed a finger to his right cheek. "You're bleeding."

"A fragment from one of the stun grenades must have caught me. Secretary Holmes, are you okay?"

She sat a few feet away from him, clearly trying to gather herself together. She nodded. "Yes. I'm fine."

"Madam Secretary, Lt. Governor Sheridan, Mrs. Sheridan, I'm Special Agent Brad Tucker. If you could go with SA Evers here, we'd like to have the EMTs evaluate you and then evacuate you from the building."

Reece got to his feet, then gave Kara a hand, while SA Tucker helped Secretary Holmes to her feet. He held out his hand first to Tucker and then Evers. "Thank you."

"You're welcome, sir."

"I promised a friend, the man who was just killed, that I'd watch over his wife." Reece still couldn't believe Hunter was gone. "She comes with us."

SA Evers grinned. "You'll be happy to know Hunter's okay."

"What?" Kara's eyes went wide.

"He's alive?" Reece asked.

"We just found that out ourselves." Evers pointed toward the doors. "See?"

Hunter entered the ballroom, a hard look on his face, his gaze moving over the room searching for Sophie.

Reece felt a dark weight lift off his chest. "That son of a bitch!"

Kara smiled, gave a laugh. "Oh, thank God!"

"He certainly has courage," Secretary Holmes said.

"Yes, ma'am, he does," SA Evers said. "Now, if you could please follow me."

Reece realized the agents wouldn't start clearing everyone else until they were safely away. He wrapped his arm around Kara's shoulder and followed Evers, who led them through the main doors and down the stairs, where they were checked over.

"I think you ought to be seen in the ER," one of the EMTs told Kara. "It's possible you could have a concussion or a fractured cheek."

But Kara shook her head. "I just want to go home."

Evers escorted them out into the cold night, where an armored Mercedes limousine waited for them, part of a high-security motorcade. He waited for Secretary Holmes and Kara to get inside the vehicle, then climbed in behind them, sitting beside Kara and across from Secretary Holmes.

"My wrap," Kara said as they drove away.

"Our car." Reece grinned. He took off his tux jacket and draped it around her shoulders to keep her warm.

"Let's turn up the heat." Secretary Holmes pushed buttons on a control panel, then lit up a cigarette, her hands shaking. "I hope you don't mind."

Normally, Reece would mind, but tonight…

Then Secretary Holmes took an iPhone out of its charging slot, dialed a number. "Mr. President, it's over. Yes, thank you. I'm fine. They're taking me back to my hotel now. I can't be certain, but it seemed to me that all the hostages were rescued safely. HRT did its job well—with some inside help and good local support." She smiled at Reece. "Sheridan and his wife are also safe. Sheridan handled himself admirably under pressure, sir. His courage and ingenuity helped save lives tonight."

She chatted with the president for a few more minutes, then called Ambassador DeLacy and had a similar conversation with him, the lights of Denver's streets sliding past the limo's tinted windows.

Kara nestled against his shoulder, her fingers lacing through his.

Reece wanted nothing more than to get her safely home. "How's your head?"

"It's okay. I'm fine—just tired, really."

"Are you sure we shouldn't go to the ER?"

"I just want to go home and hug the stuffing out of the kids. My mom must be worried out of her mind."

"Yeah." Reece gave her fingers a squeeze.

Secretary Holmes' hotel wasn't far from the Palace. She shook Kara's hand and then Reece's, thanked them both. "I've got my eye on you, Sheridan."

"Thank you, ma'am."

She spoke to the driver. "Take them anywhere they want to go."

Reece gave the driver their address.

He touched his fingertips to the swelling on Kara's cheek. "I'm sorry I wasn't able to stop him. I just didn't see it coming."

He was also sorry that he hadn't gotten a chance to take a swing at Moreno before HRT had ended his life. But the bastard *was* dead. That was something.

"Stop apologizing." Kara shifted in his arms, looked up at him. "I have never been more proud of anyone than I was of you tonight."

That hit him right in the chest. "Yeah?"

"You stood up to that bastard again and again, trying to protect me, Secretary Holmes, Holly, Sophie, Marc. You tried to protect all of us. I'm so glad he didn't shoot you just to shut you up."

"Or you." Reece kissed her forehead, tension he'd carried all night leaving him at an emotional edge.

The limo pulled up to their house.

Reece stepped out, took Kara's hand, walked with her to the front door, where Lily McMillan, Kara's mother, was waiting for them.

"Oh, my God! Are you okay? I've been watching the news. They haven't announced that it's over. Did you escape? Oh … What happened to your face?"

"I'm so glad to be home." Kara hugged her mother, Jakey, their old black lab sniffing around their feet, tail wagging.

Behind Lily stood Connor, Caitlyn, and Brendan, looking solemn.

"What happened, Dad?" Connor asked.

Caitlyn held fast to her teddy bear. "Why does Mommy have a black eye?"

"It's a long story." Reece hugged Connor, who was now 14, then drew both Caitlyn, 8, and Brendan, 7, into his arms. "Your grandma let you stay up this late?"

"Well, I figured …" Lily started to defend herself, then stopped, wiping tears from her cheeks. "I'm so glad you're safe. Did they get the bastards?"

"Oh, yes," Reece answered, not wanting to say more in front of the kids.

Kara smiled, tears streaming down her cheeks. She held out her arms to the children. "Come here. Oh, I missed you. For a while tonight, I was afraid I'd never see you again."

Reece's throat went tight.

23:32

"WE NEED EVERYONE TO stay down." Tuck's voice carried above the tumult. "We'll get you out of here as soon as we can. We know you've had a long night and want to go home. But we need to clear you and get those who need medical attention out the door first. Hey, Schroder, can you give Rossiter's wife a hand? She is our first priority."

"I'm on it."

All of it was just background noise to Marc. He pushed his way through the room, looking for Sophie. He found her sitting near Kat, Matt's arm around her shoulders, the sight of her like a fist to his gut. She looked devastated, confused, her face tear-stained, grief and shock plain on her face. He called to her. "Sophie!"

It was Joaquin who heard him. "Hunter? *Madre de* … "

Sophie's head jerked around. Her eyes went wide. "Hunt?"

She jumped to her feet, ran to him, and threw herself into his arms, her body trembling. "Oh, Hunt!"

"It's okay. It's going to be okay." He held her hard against him, kissed her hair, her forehead, the feel of her in his arms making him whole again.

She looked up at him, her fingertips tracing his forehead, his cheekbones, his jawline, tears glittering in her eyes. "I-I thought you were ..."

"So did I." He found it hard to speak, his throat tight, a riot of raw emotions inside him. "God, Sophie."

"Is it really over?"

"Yeah."

"Thank God."

And for a moment, they stood there, Marc only vaguely aware of what was happening around them.

"*Hunter?*" Darcangelo's surprised voice came from behind him.

Marc looked over his shoulder, saw Darcangelo staring at him as if he were a ghost. "Hey, buddy."

Marc released Sophie, reached to shake Darcangelo's hand, and found himself snatched up in a crushing hug. And damned if Marc didn't hug him right back, the two of them holding each other tight.

"I thought you were ..." Darcangelo slapped him on the back a few times, then stepped away, a suspicious sheen in his eyes. "I was looking for your body, but ... Yeah ... You look pretty good for a dead man."

"I see you're running with HRT these days."

"Someone had to save your ass."

Marc chuckled. "That someone was Holly."

"What?" Sophie and Darcangelo said almost in unison.

"I was on my knees with the two of them behind me, and I thought it was over. It took a second after the shot was fired for me to realize I wasn't the one who'd been hit. Holly had come up behind them. She took out one. Andris took out the other."

Sophie called across the room to her. "Holly!"

Holly stood near Moreno's body talking with Tuck, Andris beside her. She looked over at them, smiled, her left cheek bruised and swollen.

"Thank you!" Sophie mouthed.

Holly blew her a kiss, smiled.

And then Joaquin, Matt, and Alex were there.

Joaquin clapped Marc on the shoulder. "Glad to see you're okay, man."

"Thanks." Marc reached for Matt's hand, shook it. "I know what you did for Sophie. I want to thank you. That took a lot of courage. I won't forget it."

"Yeah, bro, that took balls," Joaquin said.

Matt looked embarrassed. "I'm just glad you're both safe."

"Excuse us. Coming through."

Marc looked behind him to see two EMTs with a gurney. They'd come for Kat.

"Oh, thank God," Sophie said. "Poor Kat. I can't imagine how horrible this has been for her. She's been so brave."

Marc wiped the tears off Sophie's cheeks with his thumbs. "You've been pretty damned brave yourself."

Seeing her stand up to Moreno had taken a few years off Marc's life.

"I don't know about that." Weariness seemed to wash over Sophie, the aftermath of shock and adrenaline, and she started to babble. "We should call Tessa, tell her what's happened, let her know we're going to be late."

"She knows."

Sophie went on. "We need to get you to a hospital, and I should help Kat or go in to the office and help Tom get a package of articles ready for tomorrow's front page. I know he's going to want to—"

"Sophie," Marc said, cupping her face in his hands, "you've done enough. Kat is with her husband, two EMTs, and HRT's medic. We're going to wait to be cleared, and then we'll head over to pick up the kids."

Then he remembered she didn't know about Addy. "Addy has an ear infection."

"What? Oh! God. Poor thing!"

"Schroder, the medic over there, paid a house call and took her antibiotics and eardrops. Tessa has taken great care of her."

"How do you know all this?"

He told her about his cell phone contact with Irving and Darcangelo and how Andris and Tower had arrived in one of Cobra's helicopters and they'd all gotten patched into HRT's coms.

"Hey, Hunter. I'm glad to see you upright and breathing." Tuck shook first Marc's hand and then Sophie's. "It's a pleasure to meet you, ma'am. I'm Tuck."

Marc recognized him by his voice and was glad to put a face with the name. "You and your boys get the job done."

"I could say the same for you. You are sheer hell in a fight. I heard you served as a sniper with Special Forces."

Marc nodded. "That was a long time ago."

"Ever think of joining the Bureau and trying out for HRT?"

Marc wrapped his arm around Sophie's waist. "Thanks, but I'm happy with what I have here in Denver. Besides, I'm getting too old for this shit."

Tuck looked at the duct tape on his ribs. "I've cleared the two of you. There's an ambulance waiting to take you to the ER. It looks like you're a little worse for the wear."

Marc looked down, saw blood still oozing from beneath his duct tape. Tuck was probably right. He needed to make a trip to the ER.

From behind them came Tom's voice. "I know everyone is tired. We've all had one hell of a night. But we've got a story to tell, and we can tell it like no one else."

Sophie turned to listen.

"That's right," said Baird. "I hope that photographer got photos of—"

Tom cut him off. "Baird, you are done at the *Denver Independent*. There's not a member of the staff who will tolerate you at the helm."

Cheers and applause.

"Go to hell, Baird!" Alex shouted. "You suck."

Tom turned to the newspaper staff. "Who can help me get our story out?"

Hands shot up, and people called out, Matt, Joaquin, and Alex among those who volunteered.

"Thanks, Tuck," Marc shook the man's hand once more. He ducked down, kissed Sophie's cheek. "Come on. We're leaving. *Now*."

23:45

KAT LOOKED UP AT the ceiling as they rolled her out of the Grand Ballroom, another contraction wrapping itself around her, the urge to push overwhelming.

"Pant. Don't push," one of the EMTs said.

Why did men, who would never have any idea what it was like to have a baby, try to tell women in labor what to do?

"Tell them to *shut up!*" she growled through gritted teeth, gripping Gabe's hand tightly with hers, fear and pain making her short-tempered. "We're not going to make it."

"We'll be fine," one of them said. "University Hospital is just a few—"

"No! It's coming now!" She reached down beneath the sheet, felt inside herself. Her baby was there. "Stop! Gabe, make them stop. The baby is coming *now.*"

"Guys, this isn't going to work." Gabe stopped the gurney, called to Holly. "Hey, Holly, can you help me? Kat is having the baby now. We need a room."

How could he sound so calm when Kat was in so much pain and their baby was going to pop out of her at any moment?

He lifted her into his arms, followed Holly down the hallway to an open room, Kat resting her head against Gabe's chest, fighting to ignore the fear that had consumed her since her water had broken.

"Schroder, stay here," Gabe said. "You other guys, just wait in the hall. She's not used to having men around when she has a baby."

"What should I do?" Holly asked.

"Just hold her hand, be there for her," Gabe answered.

Holly's fingers closed over Kat's, gave them a squeeze.

If anything had gone wrong... If her baby hadn't made it...

Fear snaked through her, left her feeling sick.

Gabe tore into a packet of sterile gloves. "I'm going to check you, okay?"

Kat nodded, bending her knees and parting her thighs for him.

He gently felt inside her. "Yeah, the baby's right here. It's a frank breech. Do we have a Doppler?"

One of the EMTs in the hallway said they did, and Schroder went to get it.

But there wasn't time.

The next contraction came, compelling her to push with all her might. She felt the baby move down, felt it stretching her.

"It's a girl," Gabe said. "Keep pushing. That's right. Great, Kat! You're doing great, sweetheart."

Kat took a breath and pushed again, pain seeming to tear her apart.

"Oh, my God!" Holly said.

"I've got one leg out... and there's the other one." Gabe laughed. "She's alive. She's okay."

Kat opened her eyes. "She ... she is?"

Gabe smiled. "She's kicking, and I can feel her little heart beating against my palm. We just need to get her out."

Relief, better than any anesthetic, washed through Kat.

Her baby was alive.

She rested, took deep breaths, and when the next contraction started, she pushed—hard.

"That's a shoulder, and another shoulder," Gabe said. "We're just going to let her rest here for a second. Sorry. I know this must hurt like hell."

Kat fought not to scream, the pain and pressure overwhelming.

"I'm going to reach inside you now and try to lift her chin."

She felt Gabe's fingers inside her.

"Okay, now push."

Kat pushed and...

The baby was out.

"My baby!" Kat reached down, and Gabe lifted their new little daughter into her arms, a wide smile on his face.

The baby's eyes were open, but she wasn't crying.

Kat rubbed her with her hands, spoke to her in Navajo. "Cry for me, little one."

"Schroder, can you grab the oxytocin? Also, we'll need a blanket, and I'd like to give the baby some oxygen."

"You got it."

He reached up with a cloth and rubbed the baby vigorously. "She's okay, Kat. She's just a little stunned. You weren't expecting to be here so soon, were you, angel?"

"Happy Birthday, baby girl." Tears streamed down Holly's cheeks. "Oh, she's beautiful and ... so tiny."

She *was* tiny, but then again she was five weeks early.

Gabe took off the gloves and gave Kat a shot in the thigh, explaining what he was doing to Holly. "Oxytocin. It helps prevent postpartum hemorrhage."

Then he held a tiny oxygen mask over the baby's face. "She's pinking up, aren't you, my little Christmas angel?"

"Can you help me pull down my dress?" Kat asked Holly. "I want to hold her against my skin where it's warmer."

Holly unzipped Kat's gown and pushed it down over her shoulders, then unfastened her bra.

Kat held her baby against her breasts, stroked her dark hair, found herself sharing a smile with her husband, euphoria washing away hours of pain and uncertainty. "Isn't she beautiful?"

Gabe nodded, a sheen of tears in his eyes, one of his hands holding the baby's. "She's perfect."

"She looks just like Alissa—only smaller," Holly said, taking one of the baby's tiny hands. "Look at her little fingers."

Gabe spoke quietly to Schroder. "We can deal with the afterbirth and cord en route or at the hospital. I think we're good to transport, but it's bitter cold out there. Do they have heated blankets in the ambulance?"

Kat was so absorbed in her little girl that she was all but unaware of the other things going on around her. Gabe draping a warm blanket around her shoulders. Holly walking beside her as they left the room. Gabe, Schroder and the EMTs pushing the gurney toward the elevator. Men in body armor moving aside for them, smiles on their weary faces. Cheers as Gabe announced to everyone that they had a little girl.

"Congratulations, Rossiter!" said a man in tactical gear. He'd removed his helmet, his dark blond hair damp with sweat. "The name's Tuck, ma'am. Your husband did some fine work for us tonight. Congratulations on your little daughter."

"Thank you." Kat had no idea what Tuck was talking about or who he was or who any of these men were. It was as if she'd just woken from a nightmare and found herself in a strange world.

One of them, the tallest one, stepped backward as the gurney rolled past him.

"Bauer, man, don't faint on me," Schroder said to him. "It's just a baby."

Gabe shook Schroder's hand. "Thanks for what you did tonight."

"Hey, it was an honor. I just helped a man catch his own baby. It's not often I get to do something like that. Congratulations."

And then they were in the elevator.

"Do you mind if I ride with you to the hospital?" Holly asked, rubbing her temple. "Nick can't get away quite yet, but I need to get to the ER."

It was then Kat remembered that Holly had been grazed by a bullet.

She tore her gaze away from the baby and really looked at her friend. "Oh, God! What happened? You've got bruises on your face."

"Long story," Holly said, not bothering to explain.

01:03

MEGAN SAT ON THE sofa beside Nate, Jack, Janet and Natalie sitting across from them. Up on the screen, Laura Nilsson was reporting on the arrest, trial, and sentencing of Oscar Moreno Ortíz, the bastard at the heart of all of this.

"Zach is with that SOB right now," Natalie said, a hint of worry in her voice.

She and Zach lived close to the Cimarron, and she'd come over to wait out the night with Megan and the others, not wanting to be alone.

"That man of yours knows what he's doing," Jack reassured her.

Up on the screen, Laura went on. "Ortíz is serving two consecutive life sentences at ADX outside Florence, Colorado."

The screen cut away to images of the prison and then one of the prisoner cells, the sight making Megan's stomach knot. She'd vowed never to see the inside of a prison again, and that included glimpses on the television screen.

She stood. "Does anyone want tea or hot cocoa?"

"I'd love more mint tea, please," Natalie said. "Thank you."

Megan walked to the kitchen, blocking out the sound of the television and with it the description of the prison. Apart from the TV, the house was quiet. They'd long since put the kids to bed, Aiden—Zach and Natalie's little boy—sleeping in an extra crib Nate had set up in one of the guest rooms.

She felt Nate come up behind her.

"I'll give you a hand," he said.

"You think I can't boil water?" She refilled the kettle, set it on the stove.

"Maybe I just want to get you alone." He turned on the burner, got the box of mint tea down, and set it on the counter. "How are you holding up?"

"I'm okay." She got down a fresh mug for Natalie and one for herself.

Nate took the mugs from her hands, put them aside, and drew her into his arms. "I know tonight must have dredged up a lot of unwelcome memories."

"Yeah, I guess it has." She closed her eyes, but that didn't stop the images from flowing through her mind.

Donny forcing her and Emily down into the dark basement. Donny threatening to kill Emily if Megan didn't get money for him. Donny pressing a gun to her face, trying to tear off her pants. Gunshots. Blood.

"Hey, you're trembling."

"I must be a wimp. Marc and Sophie's lives are on the line tonight. I shouldn't be thinking about myself."

"Hey, stop." Nate lifted her chin. "What happened that night was pretty damned awful. It would be strange if this didn't bring up that experience for you."

"You are always so nice to me."

"I love you." He smiled down at her, his blue eyes warm with concern. "You're not alone with this."

He ran his thumb over the curve of her lower lip and kissed her. It was a sweet kiss, slow and soft, the contact momentarily driving all other thoughts from her mind. When her cell phone rang, she nearly jumped out of her skin.

She slid the phone out of her pocket, looked at the display. "It's Marc."

"Hey, kiddo. I just called to say it's over. I know you've probably been following things on TV. I didn't want you to worry. The bad guys are dead. We're safe."

"Oh, thank God!" Megan pulled the phone away from her ear, relief like honey in her veins. "It's over! They're safe."

Cheers and clapping came from the living room.

"Are you okay? How is Sophie?"

"She's shaken up, but she'll be fine. We're on our way to the ER."

"The ER? Are you hurt?"

"I caught a round on the left side of my rib cage. It's nothing serious, but they'll probably clean it and give me a few stitches."

"You were shot?"

"Grazed."

Megan didn't want to think about how close he'd come to being killed. "Tessa said you got away, that you were helping SWAT from the inside."

"I'll have to tell you about it some other time." He sounded exhausted.

"Was anyone killed?"

"Six security guards were killed at the start, and ten others were wounded. You probably heard about that. All of the hostages made it out safely. Oh, Kat had her baby right as it all came to an end—a little girl."

Megan wanted to hear more, but she knew Marc needed rest. "Give Sophie a hug for me, okay? Take care of yourself."

"You, too. Go to bed, and stop worrying."

Her big brother knew her too well. "It's a sister's privilege to worry, especially when she has a brother as awesome as you. I love you, Marc."

"Love you, too, kiddo. Goodnight."

She disconnected, gave Nate a quick hug, then went to share what Marc had told her with the others.

"Well, I'm feeling like something a bit stronger than coffee or tea," Jack said when she had finished. "What do you say I break out the McCallan Rare Cask?"

Nate grinned. "Count me in, old man."

"Yes, please," said Janet.

"Me, too," said Natalie.

"I'll stick with tea," said Megan.

She didn't drink.

"I guess that means I'll be hearing from Zach soon." Natalie gave Megan a hopeful smile. "Thanks for letting me stay here with you all."

"No thanks are necessary." Jack walked over to the bar, started to pour his best scotch into crystal tumblers. "It's been a pleasure having you."

Then from the television screen, Laura announced the good news. "We've just gotten word that the hostage standoff at the Palace Hotel is over, and the hostages have been rescued. This is confirmed. The standoff is over. All of the hostages have been freed with no fatalities. We're told

that Secretary Holmes is safe. We'll have more updates as our coverage
continues."

Megan knew Laura better than most people. Javier and Nate were best
friends, after all, and Laura and Javier spent a lot of time at the ranch.
Megan could see beneath Laura's calm, professional exterior to the
overwhelming relief she felt knowing her friends were safe.

Jack raised his glass. "To happy endings."

"Happy endings."

01:15

ZACH COULD SEE THE lights of ADX in the distance. At any moment,
Ortíz would see them, too, and realize that he was headed back to his cell.
That was the moment this mission would become dangerous. Given that
Zach had spent the past couple of hours listening to Ortíz rave on about the
women he was going to fuck, the drugs he was going to do, the food he
was going to eat, and the people he was going to kill once he got home,
Zach was looking forward to a change of pace.

"Fuckers like you, McBride—I'm goin' to put a bounty on their
heads. I'll pay two-thousand dollars a pop to anyone who wants to knock
them off. I'm gonna—" His words faded, his gaze focused on the lights
ahead of them. "That's … That's the prison! You're supposed to be takin'
me to my cousin in Denver."

"I guess we made a wrong turn." Zach braced for his reaction, but
when it came it wasn't what he'd expected.

"¡Hijueputa!" Ortíz lunged at the pilot, kicked the cyclic forward,
causing the helo to lurch forward, nose pointed toward the ground.

He was trying to bring them down, trying to kill himself.

Zach reached into his pocket, activated the vest.

Ortíz screamed and collapsed onto the floor.

The pilot grabbed the cyclic and quickly regained control. "Are you crazy?"

"What the hell was that?" Ortíz demanded. "What did you do to me?"

Zach pulled the remote out of his pocket. "Remember that vest? It's called a stun vest. I push this button, and electricity hits your body through hidden electrodes. Great invention."

Ortíz glared at him. "That's cruel and unusual punishment."

"Here we go." Zach rolled his eyes. "Listen to the murderer talk about what's cruel and unusual."

The other DUSMs laughed.

"My cousin is going to kill all those hostages. Once he figures out—"

Zach leaned down. "Your cousin is dead, along with all his men."

"No!" Ortíz sat up, swung for Zach.

Zach pushed the button again. "I can do this all night."

They landed a few minutes later. A team of correctional officers was waiting to take Ortíz back into custody.

Zach watched as Ortíz was shackled and led away.

He shouted, struggled. "I can't go back, McBride! You don't know how bad it is here! I can't go—"

Heavy steel doors closed behind him, cutting off the sound of his voice.

And that was the last anyone would hear of Oscar Moreno Ortíz.

Zach pulled his cell phone out of his pocket, called Natalie. "Did I wake you?"

"We've been watching the news. I thought I'd hear from you soon." The sweet sound of her voice was like a balm, an antidote to the darkness of the world. "When will you be home?"

"We need to refuel and fly back to Denver, and then I'll have the drive up to the Cimarron from the airport. I'm guessing about three hours."

"Have a good flight, and drive safely. I miss you."

"I miss you, too." God, did he ever.

He disconnected, slipped the cell phone back into his pocket, and headed back outside into the cold. He was going home.

CHAPTER FIFTEEN

02:30

Nick sat next to Holly's hospital bed, watched her sleep. She'd been asleep when he'd arrived, and he didn't want to wake her. A CT scan had showed that she had a hairline skull fracture where the bullet had struck—news that had driven home for him how very close he'd come to losing her. Again.

His cell phone rang. He'd forgotten to silence it.

His parents.

He walked out into the hall and answered, spoke quietly in Georgian. "It's late. What are you doing still awake?"

"We wanted to hear about Holly."

He'd forgotten to update them after getting to the hospital. "The doctors say she's going to be fine. She's got a small skull fracture and a concussion. They're keeping her overnight just in case. She's sleeping now."

"That poor girl!" his mother said. "How could such a thing happen?"

And because some part of him needed to talk about it, he told them the whole story—why Holly had been at the party, how she'd realized they were about to be attacked, how she'd pulled the fire alarm, almost certainly saving lives. He told them how he'd heard she was "down" and had endured what felt like an eternity wondering whether she was dead. And he told them how she'd done what she could to distract Moreno, bringing his rage down on herself and almost paying with her life. He left out only the argument they'd had before the party.

"That girl has more courage than ten men and more lives than a cat," his mother said. "She gives me gray hair."

"The two of you make a good team, yes?" said his father. "I'm proud of you both. We are all proud of you."

In the background, he heard his brother Michael. After his parents had heard the news, the entire family—or at least everyone who lived within driving distance—had converged at his parents' house to wait out the night together, lighting candles and saying prayers for Holly.

"Your brother wants to know if you are the one who killed this Moreno."

"No, I'm not. One of the Hostage Rescue Team guys got him. I did take out the man who tied Holly up and hit her."

"Nick?" Holly's voice came from behind him.

She stood in the doorway in her bare feet and hospital gown.

"Hold on," he said to his parents. "You shouldn't be out of bed. Come."

He walked with Holly back into the room, helped her get settled in bed, then drew up her blankets. He would have disconnected, but he knew his parents wanted to speak to her. He handed her the phone.

"Please tell me you haven't been waiting up all night, Mama," Holly said.

The smile on her face told Nick that his parents had set Holly straight on that score. Worrying and staying up half the night was what one did when a family member was in trouble—at least in the Andris family.

"Yes, I'm fine. I've got a headache, but that's all. No, they didn't have to shave off my hair." Holly bit her lip, clearly trying not to laugh. "I'm glad about that, too. Yes, it was scary. Nick watched over me. He saved my life. Yes, he is. I love him. Okay. Tell everyone hello for me. Give them my love, and thank them for their prayers."

She disconnected, handed him the phone. "I can't believe they're still awake."

"You mean a lot to them." Nick slid the phone back into his pocket, took her hand. "You mean a lot to me."

She smiled. "Thanks for the roses."

The bouquet—a dozen red roses from the grocery store—sat on her bedside table next to the bouquet of yellow tulips.

"You're welcome." He eyed the yellow tulips. "Who gave you those? There wasn't a card."

"You looked?" Holly raised an eyebrow. "They're from Derek. He stopped by to check on me, then told me not to use this as an excuse to ask for extra time off."

"What a joker." Nick grinned. He knew Javier had already given Holly the rest of December to recuperate, longer if she needed it.

"What took you so long? Was there a long debriefing?"

Nick shook his head. "I was busy getting my ass chewed by HRT's commander. He wanted to know why I had ignored direct orders not to intervene on Hunter's behalf and then why, after ignoring those orders, I hadn't told them what we'd done or let them know Hunter was alive. Then he thanked me and congratulated the two of us on a job well done."

Holly sank back onto her pillow. "That was the worst holiday party *ever*."

Yes, it certainly had been.

She smiled. "Do you know what surprised me most tonight? Tom's apology."

The old hardass had shaken Holly's hand and apologized, admitting that he might have been too harsh when he'd fired her. Then he'd invited her to stop by the newsroom to visit once in a while.

Nick chuckled. "Too bad Joaquin didn't get a photo of that."

Cut the small talk. Get to the point.

It was Nick's turn to apologize.

"I'm sorry, Holly. I'm sorry I pushed you about having kids. I'm sorry I got angry and sharp with you. I've spent every minute since then wishing I'd handled things differently."

02:46

HOLLY'S VISION BLURRED. "I'm sorry I'm making this so complicated—the whole baby thing. I'm … I'm just afraid."

He frowned. "Of what?"

"Pain. You know I don't like pain or needles or any of that."

He gave a thoughtful nod, as if he understood that at least.

"I'm afraid of something going wrong with me or the baby."

"I hadn't thought about that. I guess I just see everything turning out perfectly like it's supposed to."

"You know life isn't like that."

"You're right."

"But the hardest part of it is that I'm afraid that I'll be an … *awful mom*." Her voice quavered on those last words.

And that right there was the heart of it.

Understanding dawned on Nick's face. He got up from the chair, sat on the edge of the bed, tucked a strand of hair behind her ear. "You are too full of love and humor and kindness to be an awful mom."

She sniffed. "You think so? Even with the parents I had—a mom who never cared about me and a father who…"

She didn't want to think about her father.

He wrapped his arms around her and drew her against the hard wall of his chest. "You have the biggest heart of anyone I know. You almost died tonight trying to save people's lives. You could have run out of that hotel and called 911 from the street, but instead you kept trying to raise the alarm, texting your friends, warning the guards, and finally pulling that damned fire alarm."

"I just did what anyone would do."

Okay, anyone with a little training.

He shook his head. "That's not true."

She looked into his eyes, tried to see what he saw in her, but couldn't.

He tipped her chin up. "You're going to make a wonderful mother—whenever you're ready."

He was letting her off the hook. He wasn't going to make this an issue. She could decide in her own time.

"Oh, Nick. Do you mean it?"

"Yes." He nodded. "There was a while tonight when I didn't know if you were dead or alive. It became crystal clear for me that you are the most important person in my world. I'd rather go without kids than live my life without you."

Holly took this in, his words warming her. "Do you truly think I'd be a good mom?"

"My mother does."

Mama Andris—mother of six, devout member of the Georgian Orthodox Church, matriarch of the family—thought Holly would make a good mother?

"She ... she does?"

"Yes—and so do I."

She lay back on the pillow, her fingers laced with his. "I was with Kat when she had the baby. It was ... *horrible*. And it was wonderful. So many things had gone wrong, but somehow it turned out okay in the end. Kat and Gabe were so happy, and the baby—she was tiny and precious and beautiful."

Nick smiled. "I'm glad they're both okay."

"You know, I was thinking." Holly looked up at him from beneath her eyelashes, gave him a sexy smile. "I was thinking that maybe I could get my IUD removed this next week, and we could start working at making a baby."

Nick stared at her. "Are you serious?"

She was. "Yeah. But we'd have to work at it.

He raised an eyebrow, smiled. "*Work* at it?"

"Yeah, you know—*work* at it." She lowered her voice. "That means *lots* of sex."

Nick's pupils dilated. He drew in a slow breath, let it go. "For now, you need to rest. Why don't you think about it? A lot of things happened tonight. Emotions are running high. I want you to be sure."

"I am." She held his hand between two of hers. "I've had a lot of adventures, but until you, I've never had a family, a real family. There are so many things that never made sense to me. I never knew why my parents had me. They've hated each other for as long as I've known them. Maybe I was an accident, or maybe … Who knows? But when I saw Kat holding her baby with Gabe standing there beside her, I finally got it. I finally understood. When two people love each other, kids are a way of building that love into something more."

She shook her head, frustrated at her inability to express what she felt. "I'm probably not making much sense."

She looked up to find him watching her.

"No, that makes perfect sense." He smiled. "But rest now, okay?"

"You'll stay with me?"

"Forever."

03:20

JULIAN WORKED WITH HRT and FBI SWAT to help them process the scene as quickly as they could. HRT oversaw the removal of the explosives, while DPD evacuated the hostages, sending anyone with injuries to one of the area hospitals, all of which had been on standby in case the worst should happen.

Around midnight, DEA showed up, as well as ATF, everyone working their own angle on this one, all of them trying to answer the same question: How had a known narco-terrorist set up an operation as extensive and lethal as this one?

"Want to ride back to the mobile command center with us?" Tuck called to him.

"Yeah. Thanks." He made sure he had all of his gear and walked down the stairs with them to the armored SWAT vehicle that waited there.

Their banter as they drove the two blocks to United Nations Park was familiar to him—the jibes and taunts that marked close friendship among men.

"Tuck and Bauer—your Laurel and Hardy routine had poor Darcangelo here thinkin' you two couldn't defuse an alarm clock," Cruz said. "You were nervous, man."

"Not really." Julian shook his head.

Cruz raised an eyebrow.

Julian held up his hands in mock surrender. "Okay, I was nervous."

They all laughed.

"Sorry about that." Tuck chuckled. "You do good work, Darcangelo."

"Thanks. Same goes. I was impressed with what I saw here tonight." Julian meant it. "Thanks for letting me be a part of it."

"We got a lot of help from the inside tonight," Evers said. "You Denver boys don't mess around. Well, I guess I can't say 'boys.' Holly Andris is something else."

Tuck grinned. "It's like I said. They took the wrong damned bunch hostage."

They stopped at the park, where DeLuca was waiting for them outside the mobile command center.

"You boys ready to get some shut-eye?" He turned to Dixon and Chief Irving and shook their hands. "You can both be proud of your men. Darcangelo, you handled yourself well. Please let your wife know that she was our game-changer tonight."

"She'll be happy to hear that, sir." God, Julian couldn't wait to hold her.

With a smile, DeLuca turned and walked with his men toward the waiting Blackhawk.

"Did you ladies remember everything?" Tuck asked.

In less than a minute, they were airborne.

"And that is how they do that," said Irving, watching the Blackhawk disappear into the darkness.

"You know, Darcangelo, I've always had a man crush on you," said Det. Wu, who'd volunteered to work through the night. "But I think these guys might have just taken your place in my heart."

Julian grinned, clapped Wu on the back. "That's fine by me."

"I'm heading home." Julian looked around, trying to remember where he'd parked his truck. "I won't be in today."

Irving nodded. "Fair enough. I imagine you and Hunter are expecting overtime and maybe a bonus."

"Hunter deserves a medal."

"Yes, he does." Irving nodded. "I'm damned glad he's still with us. That just about scared the hell out of me."

"Same here." *Jesus!*

Irving clapped him on the shoulder. "Get some sleep."

Julian located his pickup and drove past the red and green lights of the Denver City and County Building and through the empty streets. Out of nowhere his mind flashed on another early morning drive home. He'd arrested an asshole named Lonnie Zoryo and had spent the night interrogating the bastard. He'd had no idea as he'd driven on these same streets that fate had put him on a collision course with a pretty blond reporter who would change his life—or that Denver would soon become his home.

Now that pretty blond reporter was his wife. They had two kids, a nice house, good friends, even a puppy for God's sake.

Yeah, he was lucky.

He pulled into his driveway, made his way up the porch steps and unlocked the door, warm air spilling over him, carrying the scents of home—coffee, leather furniture, the pine of the Christmas tree.

He found Tessa asleep on the sofa in her clothes, a throw blanket tugged up around her shoulders, the Christmas tree still twinkling. She'd been waiting for him—not for the first time.

He slipped out of his jacket and his boots and then stripped off his weapons and body armor, tip-toeing to the bedroom to lock the weapons safely away from the kids in the gun safe. In the hallway, he caught just a glimpse of Addy and Chase, who were asleep in the guestroom. He walked to the door, peeked in.

They've taken Hunter out into the hallway to execute him.

Live shooter. I say again, live shooter. We have a shot fired.

Julian swallowed—hard. He was so damned glad they still had their father and that Sophie still had her husband.

Wired on adrenaline, he thought about slipping down to the basement for an aikido workout. But that's not what he wanted.

He wanted Tessa.

He sat beside her, ran a finger over her cheek, reluctant to wake her, but needing her just the same.

She opened her eyes, saw him, smiled sleepily up at him. "Julian."

"Hey."

She sat up, her long curls tousled from sleep. "Sophie called from the ER. It's taking longer than they thought. There were bullet fragments in Marc's wound. I told her they should just get some sleep and pick up the kids in the morning."

Julian nodded. "How's Addy?"

"The eardrops seemed to help. Nathan, the HRT medic, was great with her. He said he doesn't work with kids very often, but you would never be able to tell."

"Did you hear he helped Gabe deliver Kat's baby?"

"Really?" Tessa smiled. "Boy or girl?"

"A little girl."

"Poor Kat! That must have been a nightmare."

"Yeah." He remembered what DeLuca had said. "Supervisory Special Agent Matt DeLuca, the commander of HRT, wanted me to tell you that you were our game-changer tonight. The information you gave us about the tunnels got everyone home faster and probably saved law enforcement lives."

"Really? Wow." She smiled. "I'm glad I was able to help."

He reached out, tucked a strand of curls behind her ear, tied up in his own emotions, feeling edgy, his body tense.

Tessa seemed to sense this. "How are *you*?"

He was about to say fine, but that's not what came out. "I thought we'd lost him."

"Who?"

"Hunter."

"When he went silent on the roof?"

Tessa didn't know. Sophie hadn't told her.

Julian explained what had happened, trying to remember all the details. "DeLuca said they'd taken Hunter in the hallway to execute him, and the next thing I knew they reported a shot fired. I thought ... We all thought ..."

"I'm so sorry. That must have been so hard for you."

He tried to find the words, but couldn't, so he moved the story forward. "I didn't find out till later that the shot they'd heard had come from Holly—well, Holly and Nick. She and Andris had timed their shots so it sounded like a single blast. They took out both assholes at the exact same second."

Tessa didn't look all that impressed by this, but then she didn't know much about firearms or marksmanship. "I'm so glad they were there."

"Yeah." So was he.

"Are you hungry? Can I get you something to drink?"

He shook his head, let his fingers stroke her hair. "All I want right now is you."

04:05

THE LAST THING ON Tessa's mind was sex, but she didn't say that. She was tired and more than a little shaken by everything that had happened. But she could feel Julian's need, sense the tangle of emotions inside him. He'd done his job tonight, almost losing his best friend and risking his own life to confront the ugliness of the world.

Tonight, that ugliness had left its mark on him.

She stood, led him to their bedroom, and turned on their bedside lamp, willing herself to let everything else go and focus on the man she loved. She undressed him, first the black turtleneck, baring his chest and belly.

She splayed her hands across his chest and felt the first stirrings of desire, his pecs firm beneath her palms, his flat nipples dark like wine, dark curls scattered across soft olive skin. He held still, let her play, not rushing her, as she moved her hands over that skin, working her way down to the ridges and valleys of his belly, tracing the thin line of curls that ran from his navel to the waistband of his trousers. She unbuttoned them, tugged down the zipper, and pushed them down over his hips together with his boxer briefs, her hands sliding over the hard mounds of his bare ass.

He was already hard, his cock springing free.

She felt a flutter deep in her belly—and reached out to touch him. She knew some women didn't think a man's junk was much to look at, but she loved Julian's penis. It jutted out—erotic, primal, so incredibly sexy.

She found herself on her knees, taking him into her mouth, licking him, tasting him, stroking him. She heard his quick gasp, the breath leaving his chest in a moan, his fingers sliding into her hair. Oh, yes, she knew his body. She knew what he liked, what burned him up. She knew what made this big man beg.

She teased him with her tongue, took him deep into her mouth, then began to move her hand and mouth along his length, her hunger growing. She loved the taste of him, loved the hard feel of him against her lips and tongue.

He stilled her motions, his hands on either side of her head. "Stop. I don't want this to end before it begins."

She stood, saw that his pupils were dilated, his eyes dark, his brow furrowed—and her pulse skipped. She started to unbutton her blouse.

"Uh-uh. My turn." His fingers moved over the buttons, and then he tugged it off her shoulders and down her arms, letting it fall to the floor.

She turned to give him easy access to her bra clasp, heat skittering over her skin where his fingers brushed her as he deftly undid the clasp and tossed her bra aside.

He reached around from behind, taking the weight of her breasts into his hands and drawing her back against him, his thumbs teasing her nipples.

She rested her head against his chest, forgetting that she hadn't really been into this, his touch making her ache inside, leaving her wet.

His hands moved from her breasts to caress her belly and the curve of her hips, stopping when they found the zipper of her jeans, tugging it down, one big hand reaching inside her panties to cup her, his fingers seeking and finding her clit. Okay, so he knew her body, too, and what he was doing felt … so … *good.*

That was the thing about Julian. He never left her feeling unsatisfied, never took more than he gave. And, oh, he knew how to give.

She rocked her hips against his hand, spreading her legs as far as she could with her jeans bunched up around her thighs, her fingers digging into his forearms. She whimpered in frustration, needing more. "*Julian.*"

He turned her to face him, tore her jeans down her legs, then pulled her hard against him, his lips taking hers in a rough and hungry kiss. They fell onto the bed together, legs tangled, lips and tongues teasing, tasting. He reached between her thighs, picking up where he'd left off, drawing her nipples one at a time into the heat of his mouth with tugs she felt all the way to her womb. She spread her legs for him, gave him plenty of room, and was rewarded when he slid two fingers deep inside her.

Tessa was lost in him, lost in what he was doing to her, her body burning, wanting, needing. But he wasn't going to let her claim the orgasm she so desperately craved—not yet.

He kissed his way down her body, nibbling her heated skin, then settled himself between her thighs, parting her for his mouth. "God, you smell good."

Then he buried his face in her, teasing, licking, tasting, his fingers still busy deep inside her. Her fingers fisted in his hair, her breath coming in little moans. Then he did that thing he did—sucked her clit into his mouth, swirling his tongue over her—and she came, orgasm washing through her in a tide of bliss.

For a time, she lay there, barely able to move, her mind blank, her body floating.

Julian kissed his way back up her body, one hand caressing her, sexual heat radiating through his skin. Their gazes met, Tessa's breath catching at the need in his eyes. She reached down, took his cock in her hand, and guided him to her.

He slowly slid inside her, his eyes still looking into hers. Then he began to move, rocking in and out of her, his cock thick and hot and hard.

"Tess. My sweet Tess." The tenderness in his voice took her breath away.

She ran her hands up his chest, over the hard muscles of his shoulders, down his biceps. She'd always been in awe of his strength, more than a little amazed that a man who used his body as a weapon could be so gentle. He was the only man who'd ever loved her like this, the only man she'd ever longed for until it hurt, the only man she'd wanted to share her life with. And he'd never let her down.

He moved faster now, driving hard, thrusting deep. She lifted her legs, brought her knees all the way back, opening herself to him completely.

He moaned, his eyes drifting shut. "*Oh, Jesus.*"

She'd thought she was spent, but already she was moving toward another orgasm, his strokes hitting that sweet spot inside her. She wrapped her arms around him, drew him down until his heart was beating against hers, skin against sweat-slick skin, chest hair rasping against sensitive nipples. "*Yes!*"

Pleasure crashed in on her again, sweeping her away, but this time, it took him, too, and he shook apart in her arms.

They held each other after that, Julian tracing lazy lines over her skin, Tessa's body replete, drowsiness stealing over her.

"You always bring me back. No matter what happens, you bring me back. You make me feel clean again. You know what that is?"

Of course, she did.

"It's love." She was so very sleepy.

"It's a miracle."

04:30

SOPHIE WATCHED MARC DOZE. They'd given him a big dose of IV pain meds when they'd brought him back from the procedure room. Now, white bandages covered the left side of his rib cage, the IV in his left hand delivering antibiotics.

The wound was much worse than Sophie had thought it would be. He must have been in pain all night, but he hadn't let it slow him down. The doctor had removed five lead bullet fragments and bits of cloth from the wound, and stitched him up.

Marc had watched them explore his torn tissue with the dispassionate interest of someone who'd clearly spent too much time in law enforcement. "Oh, yeah, look at that. That was some seriously cheap-ass ammo."

Cheap or not, that bullet had nearly ended his life.

Oh, Marc.

God, he was precious to her.

He was so tall his feet stuck out of the bottom of the gurney, his shoulders almost as broad as the thin mattress. His tattoos—the US Army eagle and shield on his right biceps and the Celtic armband that wrapped around his left—stood out against the bright white of the sheets, the blanket bunched around his hips. Other people saw the exterior. They saw a big, powerful man with tats and an attitude. But to her he seemed vulnerable.

Was he cold?

She stood, pulled the blanket up over his chest, her gaze falling on the round bullet scar on the right side of his chest. That bullet had been meant for her. But he had taken it, almost dying to protect her.

And tonight again...

Somewhere nearby, a door slammed, the sound making Sophie jump, her pulse racing. She took a deep breath, wrapped her arms around herself, events of the night seeming to press in on her.

The blast of the gunshot. The brutal crush of grief. Moreno's cruel laughter.

Tears pricked her eyes. She fought them back, refusing to give in. If she started crying, she might not stop. Besides, it was over. Moreno was dead. Marc was alive and whole. She had so many reasons to be grateful. She should be smiling.

What was wrong with her?

She'd thought he was dead. For long, terrible minutes, she'd believed that the man she loved was dead.

A warm hand touched her arm. "Hey, sprite. You're crying."

Sophie smiled, wiped her tears away, and dropped the tissue in the trash. "I'm just ... overwhelmed, I guess. Are you in pain?"

Marc shook his head. "They numbed me up pretty well, and with all the pain meds in my bloodstream—hell, I can't feel it at all."

When the anesthetic wore off, it would be a different story.

"But don't change the subject." His fingers clasped hers. "You're crying."

"No, I'm trying valiantly *not* to cry." She turned her face away, studied the fluorescent light above his bed.

"I'm sorry. I know you had a really rough night."

She shook her head. "A rough night is waiting for you to come home from a raid. Or being awake with a sick kid. Or having the furnace go out when it's fifteen below. This wasn't a rough night. It was ... It was a *nightmare*."

Oh, God. Here she went. Tears.

Damn!

He released her hand, reached up, ran his big thumb over her cheek. "I'm sorry I didn't get you out of that place in time to—"

"Don't you dare apologize. You had no idea what was happening. You did everything you could to keep me safe. It's just that ..."

His dark brows bent in a frown. "It's just ... what?"

"I thought you were dead!" The tears flowed freely now. "I heard that gunshot, and I thought you were dead. God, it hurt *so* much. I couldn't figure out why I was still breathing and alive, because ... because the pain was *awful*. I don't even know how many minutes went by, but those were the worst minutes of my life. And now I keep hearing that gunshot in my mind and feeling it in my chest ..."

He sat up, kicked his legs over the side of the bed, and drew her into his arms, holding her, whispering soothing words, one big hand cupping the back of her head, his lips finding her temple. She wrapped her arms around him, sobbed out her grief against his chest, the pain caused by those terrible minutes slowly lessening.

He drew back, handed her a tissue, pressed kisses to her forehead. "When they took me out onto the balcony to shoot me, there was a moment when I realized this was it. Game over. But dying to save your life—well, that felt like a fair trade to me. I was only sorry to be leaving you so soon. Everything I am is because of *you*, Sophie."

She sniffed, shook her head. "That's not true."

"Oh, yes, it is. If not for you, I'd still be in prison. I probably wouldn't have gone into Special Forces."

"Really?"

"You told me to reach for the stars, remember? So I did."

She didn't know what to say. She'd never realized her words, spoken when she was just sixteen, had had such an impact on him.

He went on. "I wouldn't be a father. My Chevy would belong to some … weirdo."

This made her laugh.

Then he kissed her, a soft kiss, sweet and tender. "Tonight is going to be with us—with all of us—for a long time."

CHAPTER SIXTEEN

Sunday dawned, snowy and cold, on a city in mourning. By order of the governor, flags were lowered to half-mast. And the residents of Denver pulled together.

Signs appeared in people's yards and on social media reading, "Mile High Strong," "God Bless Our Police," and "Thank you, HRT & SWAT!" Some locals organized a blood drive in honor of those wounded in the attack. Others set up a bank account for donations for the families of the slain security guards.

The Denver Police Department worked tirelessly to get cars, cell phones, wallets, and coats back to their owners. A few officers were assigned to retrieve the bits and pieces of a certain Browning M2 machine gun from the rooftop of the hotel and the surrounding streets, which were still cordoned off to traffic.

The Palace Hotel expressed its condolences to the families who'd lost loved ones, offered moral support to those who'd been injured, and gave thanks to all the law enforcement agencies involved. Then it closed its doors to repair the damage.

On Sunday night, a candlelight vigil was held in Civic Center Park for those who had died and been wounded in the attack, numbers swelling into the thousands despite the snow and cold. At 7:28 p.m., the exact moment when the first shots were fired, the holiday lights on the Denver City and County Building were dimmed in memory of the men who'd given their lives.

The television news media covered the story nonstop, but it was Laura Nilsson's coverage that captured the nation's heart. She flew to Denver and put together a series of interviews, which she titled "Portraits of Courage," that told the stories of some of the heroes of that terrible night, including the mother who'd been forced to give birth in the midst of terror and death. By Monday, that tiny baby had become a symbol of survival—new life in the face of tragedy.

One of the tabloids latched onto Marc Hunter and Gabe Rossiter's stories, running it with the headline "'Die Hard' in Denver." That, too, ended up on social media, much to the consternation of both men, who didn't like being singled out when so many had done so much to get the hostages out alive.

One name did not appear in the papers: Holly Andris. Cobra staff worked overtime to keep her identity and her face out of police reports and news stories. When Governor Thyfault announced late Monday that he would be awarding Holly, Marc Hunter, Gabe Rossiter, and Lt. Gov. Sheridan the state's Medal of Valor, its highest award, at a public reception in January, Derek Tower met privately with him to impress upon him how important it was for Cobra employees to keep low profiles. It was agreed she would receive her award at a private dinner at the governor's mansion with her husband, the other medal recipients, and Ambassador DeLacy in attendance.

Then Tuesday came, and it was time to bury the dead. Four of the security guards who'd been killed were employees of the Bureau of Diplomatic Security, which oversaw protection details for the Secretary of

State. Their funerals were held in Washington, D.C., with Secretary

Holmes and the President in attendance. But two had been Denver boys,

hotel employees with family and friends in Colorado.

Lt. Governor Reece Sheridan was asked to deliver the eulogy at a

joint service for the two men, which was held in Cathedral Basilica of the

Immaculate Conception, the only church capable of seating the thousands

of people who were expected to attend and pay their respects. Reece spoke

of the men's dreams and aspirations, of the love they had for their friends

and families, of their courage the night of the attack. His closing words,

delivered with a quaver in his voice, made the all the news networks.

"The Bible says there is no greater love than to lay down one's life for

one's friends. But we weren't their friends. We were strangers to them.

Noah James Mason and Malik Rashad Davis used the last minutes of their

lives to save strangers. None of us gets to choose when or how we're going

to die. All we get to decide is how we face our end. Noah and Malik chose

to die as heroes. We will not forget them … or their sacrifice."

Though the two men hadn't been law enforcement officers in the strict

sense, they were laid to rest with full honors, the Denver Police

Department and other agencies treating them like brothers in blue,

following their hearses with a police motorcade, lights flashing. Despite

the cold, people lined the streets to show their respect, waving Colorado

and US flags as the motorcade passed.

That night, snow fell thick, blanketing the men's graves.

And stillness fell over the city.

MEGAN SAT WITH NATE, Jack, and Janet late on Christmas Eve after

the kids had been put to bed, watching a recording of Laura's interview with Kat on the screen of their home theater. Laura and Javier were there, too, having decided to spend the holidays at the Cimarron, where they could be closer to their friends.

"And the words of the song just came to you?" asked Laura on the screen, looking beautiful, polished and professional, her pale blond hair in a sleek braid.

"Yes." The camera moved in on Kat and the newborn baby in her arms.

"Did that help you deal with your fear and the pain?"

"Among the Diné, we believe songs have power. When we build a home for people—a *hogaan*—we sing it into being. Our healing ceremonies are all songs. I believe the words came to me at that moment to give me the strength I needed."

Janet shook her head. "I cannot imagine what she went through."

"She is incredibly strong," said the live Laura on the sofa.

"Look who's talking," Javier muttered in his wife's ear.

Jack paused the playback. "I think we should invite them up on Saturday, have a get-together. We can fire up the grill, hitch Buckwheat up to the sleigh, get out the sleds, maybe break out some skis."

"You want to invite Kat and Gabe over to grill, sled, and go for a sleigh ride?" Nate asked. "Do you think they'd be up for that with a new baby?"

"Not just Kat and Gabe, knucklehead." Jack chuckled. "The whole gang."

"Given what they've been through, is now a good time?" Janet asked.

"I think now is the perfect time." Jack sipped his scotch. "Let's give them a chance to get together, to sort things out, to enjoy some fresh air away from the city. What do you think, Laura? You've spent time with most of them."

Laura looked startled to be put on the spot. "Well ... I think they might enjoy it. There's something very healing about this place."

Megan knew that was true.

"I figure they've done their part," Jack said. "They gave everything they had and more. They're our friends. Now let's do our part."

"All right, old man." Nate grinned. "We'll send out emails tonight."

"I'm glad that's settled," Megan said. "Now quit talking and hit play. I want to watch the rest of this before Santa comes."

Jack raised the remote, started up the program again.

Nate leaned in, whispered into Megan's ear. "You've been very naughty this year. What makes you think Santa is bringing you anything?"

She smiled, whispered back. "Santa brings me extra presents when I'm naughty."

ON SATURDAY MORNING, NICK and Holly grabbed their winter gear and headed up into the mountains. Neither of them was really in the mood for a barbecue, but since everyone in the gang was going to be there, it would give them both a chance to reconnect. Apart from Laura and Javier, they hadn't seen any of their friends since the night of the attack.

"I never get tired of that view," Holly said when they crested a hill in the road and ranch's great house came into view. "It's so beautiful."

Built of stone and logs, it was a mix of Swiss chalet and western styles with a steeply gabled roof and high windows. Several stone chimneys jutted upward, smoke curling toward the sky. The front door was set back from a portico driveway accented by a colonnade of polished logs.

They drove up to the front and parked beneath the portico right behind Marc and Sophie's SUV.

Janet answered the door, welcoming them with a warm smile. "I'm so glad you were able to make it."

She led them to the living room, where Megan was sitting with Kara, Tessa, Laura, Sophie, and Natalie, three babies playing on the floor at their feet—Jackson, Lily, and Aiden.

Megan saw them, rose, gave Nick a quick hug and then embraced Holly. But she didn't let go. Was she crying?

"Thank you both for saving my brother's life. I don't know what we would do without him."

Holly hugged her back, felt tears pricking her own eyes. She'd never had a brother or sister, but if Megan loved Marc the way Holly loved her friends, then she could understand. "I'm just happy we were there."

And she saw it in her mind again.

Marc, shirtless and shoeless on his knees, his eyes wide open. Two men behind him, one of them pointing a pistol at the back of his head.

God, she hated Moreno. That bastard!

When Megan stepped away, Sophie was there. She didn't say a word, but hugged Holly close, then gave Nick a kiss on the cheek. "You two saved my world."

"We weren't going to let them kill Hunter," Nick said.

Megan invited them to sit, but Nick excused himself to hang with the men on the back deck.

Holly sat next to Sophie, her gaze on the babies.

Well, that's new.

Normally, she didn't pay much attention to babies other than to notice that they were adorable—and loud and time consuming.

"Weren't you scared?" Megan asked her.

Holly nodded. "There was a moment when I was afraid I wouldn't reach him in time. Nick had the rifle, but I only had a pistol. I needed to get within seven yards or so to be sure I could get the shot. I kicked off my heels and ran."

Sophie was in tears. "I'm sorry. I swore I wouldn't cry, but …"

Natalie handed her a box of tissues. "You don't need to apologize."

"You all have been through hell," Laura said. "We understand that."

Then Sophie told them how she'd heard that shot and had believed that Marc was dead. "When he called my name, when I saw him again …"

"I couldn't believe it," Kara said. "Reece and I were sure he was gone, and then Evers, one of the HRT guys, pointed to the door, and there he was."

Sophie wiped the tears from her cheeks, smiled, then laughed. "When Marc explained what had happened, I shouted to Holly to thank her. She blew me a kiss like it was no big deal. Kill a bad guy, save a good man's life. It's all in a day's work."

The others laughed with her.

Holly shrugged. "It *is* my job, you know."

She picked up Jackson, who gave her a smile, showing off two tiny teeth. "Hi, little guy. Aren't you cute? How old is he?"

NICK STEPPED OUT ONTO the deck, the scent of pine and snow filling his head, some of the tension he'd been carrying since last Saturday melting away at the sight of those mountains. Maybe spending the day here hadn't been a bad idea at all.

Jack and Nate were busy setting up grills, a box of steaks from their own herd of Angus sitting on one of the tables, big patio heaters set at intervals across the deck.

Nick greeted their hosts. "Thanks for the invite."

Nate smiled. "It's good to see you again, Andris."

Jack pointed to his left. "There's beer over there in the cooler."

The *cooler* was, in fact, a big pile of snow with bottles of beer sticking out of it.

"Thanks. I don't mind if I do." He grabbed a bottle of Never Summer, twisted off the top, and took a drink.

Oh, yeah.

This was the life.

The older kids were sledding on the small hill that was the Wests' backyard, their shrieks and laughter making Nick smile. Sheridan was out there, holding Caitlyn's hand, dragging her sled back up the hill, a broad smile on his face. Corbray was down there, too, busy building a snow fort with Connor, Reece and Kara's oldest. On the other side of the yard, Tower was also building a fort and, with Emily and Brendan's help, had amassed an arsenal of snowballs.

Nick wasn't surprised to see Corbray playing like a kid, but Tower?

To the south of the house on a little rise, Ramirez was shooting photos of the mountains, Harker holding his camera bag. It had to be a relief for Ramirez to turn his lens toward the beauty of nature after photographing mayhem and violence.

McBride, Darcangelo, and Hunter sat in Adirondack chairs shooting the shit, beers in their hands, one eye on their kids.

"Hey, Andris." Hunter got to his feet, shook Nick's hand, their gazes meeting. "Thanks, man. I wouldn't be here right now if it weren't for you and Holly."

Nick knew that he had never been Hunter's favorite guy. Hunter and Darcangelo still held a grudge about the way he'd treated Holly when they'd met, and he couldn't blame them. It felt good to move up a notch in their esteem. "Hey, what are friends for? How are you feeling?"

"I'm good," Hunter said.

"Right." Darcangelo stood, dragged a chair over for Nick. "One of the kids ran over and hugged him a bit too hard, and I thought he was going to faint."

"Hey, Dickangelo, don't undermine my effort to remain manful in people's eyes."

"Dude, please." McBride shook his head. "If you're not manful, the rest of us can just give up and go home."

Nick chuckled, took a seat, shared his news. "I heard through the grapevine that Secretary Holmes has spoken to the president about awarding Hunter the Presidential Medal of Freedom."

"No shit?" Darcangelo said. "That's fantastic. Irving's going to hang some pretty ribbons on his chest, too. I'm sure of that."

"Cut it out." Hunter glared at them. "Just stop."

"I have to say that was a badass bit of marksmanship you and Holly did," Darcangelo said turning to Nick. "How did you manage it?"

And so Nick told them. He'd just finished explaining how he and Holly had timed their shots, when Matt and Joaquin trudged up the stairs, snow on their boots, the two of them laughing about something.

"There's the man," Hunter said, raising his beer to Harker.

Harker looked a bit embarrassed. "Oh, knock it off."

McBride gave a snort. "You're a hero, Harker. Just accept it."

Nick got to his feet. "Harker, Ramirez. I just wanted to thank you for taking care of Holly when she was unconscious. From what I hear, the two of you and Rossiter risked your own safety."

"Rossiter's really the one to thank for that, but you're welcome," Ramirez said, nudging Harker with his elbow. "Just say, 'You're welcome.'"

"You're welcome," Harker said, his obvious discomfort making the guys laugh.

The back door slid open, and Megan stuck her head out, a wide smile on her face. "Kat and Gabe are here with the baby."

KAT SAT ON THE sofa, Natalie and Holly making room for her, her baby daughter in her arms. Her body was still sore from giving birth, so it took her a moment to get comfortable. Gabe held a sleeping Nakai in his arms, while Alissa sat down beside her.

"Oh, she's tiny!" Natalie said. "How much did she weigh?"

"Five pounds, three ounces," Kat answered.

"Is she nursing well?" Janet asked.

"She had a little trouble at first, but she's gotten the hang of it now."

The back door opened, kids spilling inside, followed by the men.

"Whoa! Chase, Addy—slow down and stop yelling," Marc told his kids. "You don't want to scare the baby."

"Take your boots off, kids," said Reece. "You're tracking snow."

"I saw her on TV," said Maire, looking over at her father.

"Yes, you did," answered Julian, who was helping little Tristan out of his coat and snow boots. "Be quiet, okay, kids? She's sleeping."

"Have you named her yet?" Holly asked.

Kat nodded. "We named her the night she was born, but we didn't want to announce her name until we shared it with you."

She looked up at Gabe, hoped he would carry it from here. She wasn't going to be able to do this without crying.

"We want to thank all of you who helped Kat that night. Sophie, Joaquin, you were amazing. I watched while you did everything you could to help her, watching over her, trying to protect her from Moreno and his men. You're going to make a great husband and father one day, Ramirez."

Joaquin stammered. "Uh … I …"

Matt elbowed him. "Just say, 'Thank you.'"

"Thank you."

Quiet laughter.

"Holly, you held Kat's hand through the birth, even though you were injured and exhausted. It meant a lot to both of us."

"You're welcome." Holly waited a beat. "But what is the baby's name?"

Gabe grinned. "Her name is Noelle Yanaha."

"We chose Noelle because she was determined to come at Christmastime," Kat explained, her throat tight. "And we chose Yanaha as a middle name. It's a girl's name that means 'Brave' in Diné. You were all brave for me that night."

"That's so sweet," Sophie said, leaning in to get a closer look at the baby.

Gabe grinned, gave a shrug. "We thought having SophieJoaquinHollyMarcNickJulian as a middle name would be a bit awkward."

"Did they ever figure out why you went into labor early?" Sophie asked.

Kat felt her face flush.

Gabe rescued her. "The doctor said she thought it was a combination of extreme stress and too much activity."

By activity, the doctor had meant sex.

"How are you doing?" Janet asked her.

"Physically, I'm okay. I'm not getting much sleep. She's so tiny that she needs to nurse all the time. But we're doing okay. Emotionally …"

Kat wasn't one to talk about her feelings with others most of the time, but her friends had been there with her, had lived through the same nightmare. She wasn't the only one who'd suffered that night.

She did her best to put her feelings into words. "Sometimes the only way to deal with fear and pain is to open your heart to it. Grandma Alice says there's nothing we can't overcome, as long as our hearts stay open."

"Your Grandma Alice is a wise woman," Jack said.

"Can I hold her?" Holly asked.

"Of course." Kat laid Noelle carefully in Holly's arms.

"Oh, God, she's precious!" Sophie reached out, took one of Noelle's tiny hands.

"Uh-oh. I'm going to spend the rest of the month talking my wife's ovaries down," Marc muttered to Julian, who nodded in understanding.

"Hey, I heard that," Sophie said.

But she was smiling.

NATE FLIPPED THE STEAKS one at a time, his gaze on the snowball fight, which Tower appeared to be winning, with the help of several little kids who stood barely taller than his knees. "I got to hand it to you, old man. You were right."

There'd been a change in the mood of their guests through the course of the day. They'd shed some tears, shared their stories, and they all seemed to be the better for it.

His father grinned. "I usually am."

Nate had always considered his father to be wise, but he would have to give him more credence in the future when it came to touchy-feely stuff. Then again, the old man had survived two tours of duty as a Army Ranger in Vietnam, lived through Nate's close brush with death in Afghanistan, and had lost his first wife, Nate's mother, to an aneurysm. He must know something about emotions to have gotten through all that.

When the steaks were ready, they called everyone to dinner. Plates were heaped with fresh-baked rolls, mashed potatoes, salad, and roasted vegetables, the heaters turned on high to keep everyone warm as they gathered around the picnic tables.

Nate's father stood, asked for quiet. "I want to thank you all for coming up here today. It's a hell of a thing you've been through, but you all faced it head on and with courage. Your presence in our home honors us. Every one of you is a hero."

He raised his beer. "To heroes."

"Hear, hear!"

"To heroes!"

MARC SAT BACK ON the deck feeling more relaxed than he had in days. Darcangelo sat beside him, Maire asleep in his lap, wrapped in a warm wool blanket.

Above the mountaintops to the west, the setting sun had turned the clouds pink, sending Joaquin inside after his camera.

It was the first time he and Darcangelo had been alone since the attack.

The words just came. "There was a moment when I thought it was over. You know how they say your life flashes before your eyes or some shit? I realized I've had a damned good life—at least since I got together with Sophie. I wasn't afraid to die. I just didn't want to leave her so soon."

"I get that. Yeah."

"I've always known I'll die in the line of duty."

"What? Listen to that shit."

"No, I'm serious."

"Okay. You're serious."

"When that day comes—"

"*If* that day comes," Darcangelo interjected.

"—I hope you'll watch over—"

"If you finish that thought, Hunter, I'm going to put my little girl down and kick your ass." Darcangelo glared at him. "You don't even have to ask. I know you'd do the same for Tessa and the kids if anything happened to me."

"Right." Marc let out a breath. "Okay. Good."

That was settled.

Silence stretched between them.

"I thought you were gone. I thought they'd blown your head off. I came upstairs expecting to find your body." Darcangelo's voice got tight. "Man, you're the best fucking friend I've ever had. Don't let that happen again."

Marc looked at the man who was like a brother to him, their gazes meeting, words neither of them could say aloud held in that glance. "You got it."

They clinked beer bottles, drank.

The back door opened, and Joaquin came out and started taking photos. "Damn, look at that sky!"

By ones and by twos, the rest of the gang came out to see the sunset until they all stood together, staring in stunned silence at Mother Nature's handiwork.

The world was a strange place. Last Saturday, it had been terrorists and death. This Saturday, it was good friends, good food, and a spectacular sunset.

Then the last rays of the sun slipped away, the sky coming alive with stars.

"Grandpa Jack, can we show them the surprise now?" little Emily asked.

"Yes, Miss Emily, I think it's time."

The little girl ran to a switch on the side of the house and flipped it, and the forest around the house came alive with light. It was a forest of Christmas trees, dozens upon dozens of them, some with lights in mixed colors, some with strands of blue or white or red or green lights, the mountains a shadow behind them.

There were oohs and aahs.

Addy ran up to him, blue eyes that were so much like Sophie's wide with excitement. "Daddy, do you see?"

Marc pulled his daughter into his lap. "I sure do."

Yes, the world was a strange place.

But for tonight at least, life was good.

OTHER TITLES BY PAMELA CLARE

I-Team Series

Extreme Exposure (Book 1)

Heaven Can't Wait (Book 1.5)

Hard Evidence (Book 2)

Unlawful Contact (Book 3)

Naked Edge (Book 4)

Breaking Point (Book 5)

Skin Deep: An I-Team After Hours Novella (Book 5.5)

First Strike: The Prequel to Striking Distance (Book 5.9)

Striking Distance (Book 6)

Soul Deep: An I-Team After Hours Novella (Book 6.5)

Seduction Game (Book 7)

Historical Romance:

Kenleigh-Blakewell Family Saga

Sweet Release (Book 1)

Carnal Gift (Book 2)

Ride the Fire (Book 3)

MacKinnon's Rangers series

Surrender (Book I)

Untamed (Book 2)

Defiant (Book 3)

Upon A Winter's Night: A MacKinnon's Rangers Christmas Novella (Book 3.5)

About the Author

USA Today best-selling author Pamela Clare began her writing career as a columnist and investigative reporter and eventually became the first woman editor-in-chief of two different newspapers. Along the way, she and her team won numerous state and national honors, including the National Journalism Award for Public Service. In 2011, Clare was awarded the Keeper of the Flame Lifetime Achievement Award. A single mother with two sons, she writes historical romance and contemporary romantic suspense at the foot of the beautiful Rocky Mountains. To learn more about her or her books, visit her website at www.pamelaclare.com. You can also keep up with her on Goodreads, on Facebook, or by joining the private Facebook I-Team group. Search for @Pamela_Clare on Twitter to follow her there.

Made in the USA
Middletown, DE
12 December 2015